ALEXANDER KANENGONI was born in Chivhu, Zimbabwe, in 1951. He completed his primary education at Marymount Mission and his secondary education at Kutama College. He then trained as a teacher at Saint Paul's Teacher Training College.

He taught briefly before leaving the country to join the liberation war in 1974. He returned at independence in 1980 and attended the University of Zimbabwe where he majored in English literature. In 1983 he joined the Ministry of Education and Culture as Project Officer responsible for the education programmes for ex-combatants and refugees. He joined the Zimbabwe Broadcasting Corporation in 1988 where he is currently Head of Research Services.

Alexander Kanengoni's first two novels to be published were: *Vicious Circle* (Macmillan, 1983) and *When the Rainbird Cries* (Longman Zimbabwe, 1988). His collection of short stories *Effortless Tears* (Baobab Books, 1993) won him the Zimbabwe Book Publishers' Literary Awards in 1994.

ALEXANDER KANENGONI

ECHOING SILENCES

Heinemann

Heinemann Educational Publishers
Halley Court, Jordan Hill, Oxford OX2 8EJ
A Division of Reed Educational & Professional Publishing Limited

Heinemann: A Division of Reed Publishing (USA) Inc.
361 Hanover Street, Portsmouth, NH 03801–3912, USA

Heinemann Publishers (Pty) Limited
PO Box 781940, Sandton 2146, Johannesburg, South Africa

OXFORD   MELBOURNE   AUCKLAND
JOHANNESBURG   BLANTYRE   GABORONE
IBADAN   PORTSMOUTH (NH) USA   CHICAGO

First published by Baobab Books (a division of Academic Books (Pvt) Ltd),
Zimbabwe in 1997
First published by Heinemann Educational Publishers in 1998

British Library Cataloguing in Publication Data
A catalogue record for this book is available from the British Library.

Cover design by Touchpaper
Cover illustration by Ishmael Wilfred
Author photograph by Bester Kanyama

Phototypeset by SetSystems Ltd, Saffron Walden, Essex
Printed and bound in Great Britain by
Cox and Wyman Ltd, Reading, Berkshire

ISBN 0 435 91009 4

98 99 00 01 02 7 6 5 4 3 2 1

INTRODUCTION

The Zimbabwean liberation war began in the mid-1960s, climaxed in the late 1970s and ended in 1980 when the guerrillas came into 'assembly points' and the independence elections took place. The elections were decisively won by Robert Mugabe's ZANU/PF party (Zimbabwe African National Union/Patriotic Front). The party's guerrilla army, ZANLA (Zimbabwe African National Liberation Army), was operating in two-thirds of the country by the end of the war and this was the main reason for Mugabe's victory. Munashe Mungate, the central figure in this book, is a ZANLA guerrilla, as was Alexander Kanengoni himself.

In the early 1980s both scholarly works and Zimbabwean novels were concerned to celebrate the nationalist victory and in particular ZANLA's part in it. The guerrillas were seen as unblemished heroes, supported by the mass of the Zimbabwean people and in turn loyally supporting Robert Mugabe and the rest of their dedicated political leadership. This is the vision displayed, for instance, at Heroes Acre in Harare. Gradually, however, a different image of the war began to be presented, first in Zimbabwean novels and then in scholarly research. It began to be emphasised that ZANLA had not won the war by themselves: Joshua Nkomo's ZAPU (Zimbabwe African Peoples Union) and its ZIPRA (Zimbabwe Peoples Revolutionary Army) guerrillas had played an important part, particularly in the western third of the country. Both parties and armies, however, had been riven by faction and by bloody suppression of rivals. Many volunteers to the guerrilla armies had been suspected, and executed, as spies. Veteran guerrilla commanders disliked and repressed educated volunteers, who they feared would offer ideological challenges to their leadership. When ZANLA and ZIPRA met, whether in the field inside the country or in the various attempts made outside it to unite the armies, the two guerrilla armies fought each other.

Men and women who left the country for guerrilla camps in Zambia and Mozambique had terrifying experiences there – not only vicious internal feuding but also devastating Rhodesian air and ground attacks. Inside the country guerrillas fell victim to poisoned food or clothes distributed by the Rhodesian regime. In revenge many 'sell-outs' and 'witches' were killed. Recent research has vividly illuminated the particular plight of women, as volunteers to ZANLA, as refugees and as civilians in the Zimbabwean war-zones.

This new and more realistic picture of the liberation war made it hard any longer to see the guerrillas as unblemished heroes. But it also emphasised their traumatic suffering. After the war was over thousands of men and women needed healing of memories. Right up to the present *Mhondoro* (lion) spirit mediums, the shrine priests of the High God shrines in the Matopos mountains of western Zimbabwe, diviners and Zionist church leaders have been involved in exorcism of ex-combatants. The idiom of healing has been the identification, propitiation and exorcism of possessing spirits, often those of innocent victims killed during the war. In this way the horrors of the war have been remembered and represented in rural ritual as well as in novels and scholarly monographs. All these themes are represented in *Echoing Silences*, which begins with the killing of members of a defeated faction within ZANLA, contains memorable accounts of Rhodesian raids at Nyadzonia and Chimoio camps in Mozambique, and ends with an extraordinary evocation of a lion-spirit ritual.

Some comment is needed for non-Zimbabwean readers on particularly important dates and developments which feature in this book. It seems clear that Munashe joined ZANLA at a time when it was operating out of Zambia as well as out of Mozambique, probably in 1974. The Badza/Nhari revolt – the repression of which constitutes the opening scenes of the book – took place at the end of 1974. Nhari took guerrillas from the front to Lusaka where he arrested most of the military and political command; when the tables were turned Nhari and most of his followers were executed without trial. The Nhari revolt remains one of the enigmas of the war. The official version is that Nhari was a tool of Rhodesian Intelligence but there is a persistent counter-version which sees him as representing valid and serious criticisms of the army and party leadership.

The pivotal incident in the book is the killing of ZANU's chairman, Herbert Chitepo, who was blown up by a bomb at his Lusaka home on 18 March 1975. Chitepo was a barrister, writer and thinker – a model for educated volunteers to ZANLA. His death remains another mystery. The official line is that it was the work of Rhodesian Intelligence but many people believe that Chitepo was a victim of the veteran leaders of ZANLA. At any rate, the death had many important consequences. Most of ZANU's and ZANLA's leaders were detained in Zambia for the rest of 1975. Thereafter ZANLA operated exclusively out of Mozambique, leaving Zambia as a base for its rival, ZIPRA. It also left the memory of Chitepo as a martyr – a man above the sordid rivalries and crimes which followed his death. This book ends with Munashe's vision of a resurrected Chitepo, surrounded by other martyrs of the struggle, denouncing the betrayal of the revolution.

After 1975 the novel moves rapidly through the events of the war until its climax in 1980. Readers may need comment on developments which are only briefly mentioned. One of these is the emergence of ZIPA (the Zimbabwe Peoples Army), a force led by radical intellectuals among the guerrillas and supported by the front-line states (Zambia, Tanzania and Mozambique) as a preferred alternative to faction-ridden ZAPU/ZIPRA and ZANU/ZANLA. The repression of ZIPA in 1977 was another triumph for the veterans over the educated. It was at this point that Robert Mugabe (significantly not mentioned in this book) emerged as political leader of ZANU/PF and master of the ZANLA army.

Another passage in the novel relates to the long and bitter hostility between the two parties, ZAPU and ZANU, which dated back to the emergence of ZANU as a challenger in 1963, endured throughout the war, and after 1980 produced what many people have called a 'civil war' in Matabeleland. There is brief reference also to the Internal Settlement between Ian Smith and Bishop Abel Muzorewa which led to the most intense period of the war in 1978 and 1979. Muzorewa deployed 'auxiliaries', the *Pfumo Revanhu*, against the guerrillas: 'it seemed that practically the whole country was armed' (page 113).

But Munashe moves through all the events of the late 1970s in a state of disorientation, already deeply traumatised by his coerced killing of a Badza/Nhari-connected woman and her baby (described at the beginning of the book). It is with the return of this woman, in the form of a possessing spirit, and revealed by the lion medium, that the book ends.

Terence Ranger
University of Zimbabwe, 1998

Readers who wish to know more about the history of the liberation war may consult two volumes edited by Ngwabe Bhebe and Terence Ranger and published by Zimbabwe University Press and James Currey: *Soldiers in Zimbabwe's Liberation War* (1995) and *Society in Zimbabwe's Liberation War* (1996).

A glossary of Zimbabwean words and phrases used in the novel is on page 135.

PART ONE

As always, it began with the cry of a baby somewhere – perhaps in his mind – and he instinctively reached for the bottle of sedatives in his pocket – but he knew it was hopeless. The baby continued to cry and the sound drew nearer. He thought of his wife in Sakubva as he staggered to the door of his office and wobbled down the narrow corridor jostling people as he passed, his eyes glazed. Staring past him they self-consciously shook their heads, half in sympathy, half in irritation. Munashe almost ran as the crying closed in on him. He flung open the finance manager's door and shouted breathlessly above the plaintive cry:

'She is coming back sir! My wife can handle it. Please call her!'

The manager leapt up from his chair but he did not realize that the walls of Munashe's mind had already fallen in. The woman stopped digging and unstrapped the shrilling baby from her back. Munashe could see the weals through her torn blouse and he looked away. He did not want to see the emaciated baby and the mother's withered breast. And he didn't see the haggard woman rock the baby gently, whispering something in its ear. But what he did see were the tears rolling down her dejected face. And as he had done countless times since his unit arrived at the secluded base early that morning, he attempted to understand what was happening but, as on other occasions, nothing made sense and he shrugged his shoulders and looked away. He did not realize that the nightmare had not yet started. He slung his AK rifle over his shoulder and paced up and down trying to contain his anxiety. Then the security officer who had assumed command of the base since his arrival the previous day barked from the command shack under the sprawling *mukuyu* tree that he should have the

1

sell-out finish the digging so that they could get the whole damn business over and done with.

'We have more important things to do than this. There is a war to fight!' he snapped.

Munashe flinched. He watched the woman calmly strap the crying baby back on to her bruised back with a piece of soiled cloth and he saw the tears as they fell from her eyes. She reached for the crude hoe with a broken handle and began digging the hole in which she knew they intended to bury her. Munashe looked at her again and saw that her lips were moving and he wondered what she was saying to herself; perhaps she was talking to her baby. And then he wondered about the baby. What would happen to the baby?

If he had been at the camp on the previous night, he would have heard the abnormally agitated security officer argue with the base commander over what should be done with the baby. The former wanted the baby to die with the mother but the latter argued that this could not be because it had done nothing wrong; that it was the mother and not the baby who had been involved in the revolt.

'What's the difference? I don't understand what you're talking about. Where I grew up, the young of a mouse is a mouse. What is it called in your home area? And, come to think of it, where do you come from, commander?'

But Munashe had not heard this strained conversation, and as he stood in the sweltering Zambezi sun, bewildered and dismayed, listening to the agitated voice of the security officer inside the command shack, he wondered what was happening to the base commander; the man no longer seemed to have any authority. But, had he witnessed the execution of the three prisoners the night before, he would have known how utterly helpless the man was. The security officer had talked about ruthless instructions

2

from the High Command in Lusaka; instructions meant to deal with anyone remotely involved in the failed rebellion; and during all this the base commander had stood quietly by, his eyes cast down. And when the three prisoners, all male, were frog-marched behind the huge baobab, and told to dig their graves in the dark, the base commander had calmly asked whether this could not be left until the following morning.

But his words had incensed the security officer who, in a fit of rage, had shot the three prisoners at point-blank range. If Munashe had witnessed that moment of madness, he would, as so often before, have asked himself whether joining the liberation struggle had been a wise decision. But what all those present had felt was the overwhelming presence of death, their own vulnerability and the intense smell of gunpowder. There was nothing else to understand. If Munashe had been there, he would have noticed that it was then that the baby began to cry ceaselessly; and the security officer would have ordered him to help bury the dead prisoners in a single shallow grave, just a short distance away from the huge gnarled tree leaning forward like someone weeping.

Munashe wiped away the sweat that was trickling into his eyes and blurring the shapeless figure of the woman in front of him. The sound of the crying baby fused with the intense glaring heat until everything seemed a nightmare, a nightmare worse than his memory of the cave on the mountain and the foul smell of Gondo decaying beside them. He did not know that he would have felt worse if he had seen the twisted, perforated bodies of the executed men. He would certainly have cried out if he had seen how the youngest one pleaded for clemency, and how his eyes remained open after his death, as if he were still expecting to be forgiven, but nobody closed his eyelids as his mother would have done. Munashe had not see any of this because his section had

3

not yet crossed the border and made their way to the remote supply base inside Mozambique to which they had been hastily recalled. He could never have imagined that they would be caught up in this brutal confusing situation. What was happening?

And then the woman stopped digging and raised her head and their eyes met and Munashe saw that her eyes were puffed and swollen; her upper lip was torn and bleeding; and the front teeth on her lower jaw were missing. But what he saw most clearly was that her eyes were saying something which she could not put into words. Munashe quickly looked away. His eyes fell on the mound of fresh earth where the three guerrillas lay buried and his mind went back to the baby: what would they do with the baby? And then he looked back at the woman and their eyes met again. He thought she was asking what would happen to her baby and helplessly he threw his hands in the air as if to say that he too did not know what its fate would be. And the security officer saw everything through the ramshackle door of the command shack, whipped his pistol from its holster and came out of the shack, his eyes fixed unblinkingly on Munashe. The fierce sun glinted and bounced off the metal of the short butt into the young man's eyes and made him wince. The base commander saw something was wrong and followed him out.

'My instructions to you were to guard her, *killer-man*!'

Munashe opened his mouth to say something but no words were uttered. The base commander, now less agitated, stood behind the security officer. 'Since you arrived,' the security officer glared at Munashe, 'I've been watching you. I have never trusted you. You are also one of them!'

'What's happened?' the base commander asked.

'I'm not talking to you,' the security officer shouted. 'Must I keep repeating that I'm acting on instructions from the High Command? My task will be over when everyone involved with

Badza and the revolt against the struggle is brought to book. And I mean *everyone*, including *you*.' The base commander shook his head and walked away.

'I don't know anything, *chef*,' Munashe said, conscious that he was pleading.

Meanwhile, the woman kept on digging and her baby continued to cry.

'I think she has dug deep enough for two,' the base commander said. Munashe saw the leer on the security officer's face. Then the security officer wrenched the hoe with the broken handle from the hands of the beaten woman and threw it at Munashe's feet.

'Get it over with!' he snarled. Munashe looked helplessly around at the base commander who looked away and he remembered his false confession surrounded by a crowd that jeered, howling for his blood, not from anger but in desperation. And the woman stood still, rocking imperceptibly, the baby crying on her back. The base commander who seemed a little more controlled walked back from the makeshift command shack and circled the shallow pit in which the condemned woman stood, the baby crying on her back. He stopped and it appeared as if he wanted to say something to her, then he looked at Munashe, shrugged his shoulders and walked away, past the mound of drying earth where the three executed guerrillas had been buried. And then Munashe's eyes met those of the woman and he saw that she was pleading but what he could not make out was who she wanted saved: herself or the baby.

'I can't do it!' Munashe cried out involuntarily.

'This is a war,' yelled the security officer. 'Yes! Yes! You are one of them!' he concluded in triumph. The other guerrillas stood motionless, watching. The base commander walked back from behind the tree which looked like someone weeping, helplessly shaking his head.

5

'The baby hasn't done anything wrong,' he said.

'Shut up!' screamed the security officer.

'I told you yesterday that this man needs to be sent back to Chifombo for investigation,' said a female guerrilla standing next to the security officer.

'Why waste time sending him all the way back there? He's one of them. It's written all over his face.'

'I don't know what you are talking about.'

'Get on with the business, soldier!'

'Somebody help me!'

'*Pamberi nehondo*!'

The security officer grabbed the automatic rifle from the female combatant standing next to him and let out a burst of automatic fire. The deafening sound echoed across the jungle, dying out a long time later, away in the scorching distance.

One of Munashe's already painful memories about the war was the long journey from Chifombo to the war front; across the flat, monotonous Zambezi Valley, along the Zambezi River meandering lazily like a venomous snake, across a seemingly endless wilderness, through heavy forest, past the small forward supply base to which he never imaged he would have to return in such uncertain circumstances, only to be asked to kill a woman and her crying baby. Finally they had reached the border with Rhodesia; he remembered the sun, the heat, the exhaustion. They went down the escarpment from the Zambian border carrying heavy loads of armaments and food rations on their heads. By the time they got to the Zambezi River three days later, what remained were the armaments, the treacherous terrain, the little food and the scorching sun in the cloudless sky above. It was on this wicked stretch between the Zambezi and the FRELIMO base of Secunda Terçeira that desperation sneaked in.

What ran out first was water, but still they moved on, exchanging glazed looks. And when the water rations ran out, no one could touch the food because it only made them more thirsty.

Then delirium began.

That was when they forgot about the blisters between their legs, fought over their urine to quench their burning thirst and engaged in pitched battles with phantom enemy soldiers. Some died. This was how Max had died. This was how the short, bow-legged comrade that Munashe had helped to nickname Bazooka had also died.

Bazooka was a silent, thoughtful, stocky fellow in the same platoon as Munashe, who did not have any friends. Unfortunately, during military training at Chimbichimbi in eastern Zambia, his sorrowful eyes and general loneliness got him into trouble. Security suspected that he was a witch and the man was briefly detained for interrogation. Even after the torture and the beatings, they could not find any corroborative evidence and released him. But because of the sad distant look in his eyes and the fear and general uncertainty in the camp, people began to hallucinate, claiming to see strange animals that emitted strange sounds whenever they were near him and he was detained again. He was only released when he eventually confessed that he was indeed a witch and was willing to relinquish his evil ways and be rehabilitated.

Several weeks after this weird confession, Munashe found Bazooka alone and asked:

'Are you a witch?'

The man looked at him and his eyes filled with tears before he looked away and Munashe remembered how the pain of his own dilemma had utterly changed his personal perception of the struggle.

After their journey by air from Botswana to Lusaka, they were whisked away to a camp on a farm on the outskirts of the city.

They were taken in a Land Rover driven by a fat man with shifty, inflamed eyes, a khaki shirt and blue jeans; this man they later learnt was the party's chief of security. Discussion with him at the airport and in the car was curt and matter-of-fact. Munashe realized that the excitement he experienced at finally reaching the guerrilla camp had begun to ooze away. Why was the man behaving in such an unfriendly fashion? He looked at the others and saw that they felt as he did. They drove in silence all the way to the camp outside Lusaka. The Land Rover came to a halt at the main entrance to the guerrilla base and a young armed man emerged from the blind side of the vehicle and looked at them, his eyes full of suspicion. The chief of security whispered something to him, he nodded and then shouted at them to get down. There was a flurry of movement as a number of young armed men and women emerged from both sides of the entrance and formed a cordon around them. Munashe saw the open hostility in their eyes and wondered what the matter was. It was as if they had unknowingly entered enemy territory.

The young man who appeared to be their leader shouted at them to hold their luggage and form a line. His voice was cold and hostile.

'Search them!'

Munashe looked at the leader, their eyes met and he smiled timidly. This caught the young commander unaware and he looked briefly away. Then he looked back, an ugly grin on his face. Munashe looked away but he had seen that the man had squint eyes and that one of his front teeth was missing. He felt the open hostility. An ominous feeling that something sinister was about to happen assailed him.

All the small items that they had such as books, watches and money were taken away. Munashe's horror began when he was found with an old novel that he had been reading on the flight from Francistown to Lusaka. The young section commander flipped carelessly through the pages and asked:

'What's this?'

'It's a book.'

'Stupid! Do you think I'm blind?'

Munashe opened his mouth to speak but remained silent. He looked at the others he had come with and they all looked away.

'Is *this* what *they* gave you to come and spy for them?'

Munashe did not understand what was happening. 'You can take the book and read it if you want to,' he stammered.

'Who told you that I can't read?' the young commander challenged him.

Munashe opened his mouth again, and again he was silent. What was happening? They were marched to the security building not far from the main entrance. Munashe's thoughts were in turmoil. He was paralyzed with fear by what he saw inside the dilapidated security building. A young man in nothing but soiled underpants writhed in pain on the floor. His arms were tied with copper wire around the elbows behind his back so that he looked like a chicken being held by the wings; his chest was abnormally pushed out, but the people around him chatted calmly as if they were not aware of his quietly writhing presence. Munashe looked at his arms and saw the bulge that had formed between his shoulders and he wondered what wrong the young man could have done to be punished in this way.

Later they worked on Munashe and a woman tied a string around his testicles and he bellowed and in the morning his face was puffed up and his lips were torn and he could not open his eyes and because his eardrums were damaged, he could no longer hear them accuse him of being a sell-out sent by the Rhodesian Special Branch. They continued beating him, charging that all educated people from Salisbury were spies because they dined

9

and wined with the white man. He was saved several days later by an unknown man from the commissariat department who came to him in the middle of the night and said:

'Comrade, you don't know these people; they can do anything to you. Why don't you admit you are a spy to save yourself?'

He stood on the raised platform at assembly the following morning and made the astonishing confession and the ragged and disillusioned people around howled for his blood. Then the chief security officer jumped onto the platform and punched the air with his clenched fist shouting revolutionary slogans and the people thundered back and he burst into song and there was nothing to understand. He raised his hand and the people fell silent.

'The most dangerous person to our struggle is not the white man but the black enemy agent within our own ranks.' He paused and looked at Munashe. 'We will give him the long rope.'

And once again, the security chief burst into song and he began to dance as if he was possessed. As Munashe stood there, surrounded by the crowd of wildly singing people, he realized just how lonely and helpless he was. He wondered why he had joined the struggle to land himself in such a mess. And with formidable will, he detached some part of himself from the rest of his body and placed it outside the crowd to watch the painful drama as it happened to him. Would he come out of it alive?

'I know you are not a witch,' he assured the stocky fellow and the man wiped the tears from his eyes and looked at him suspiciously. 'It also happened to me,' Munashe said.

And then one day, Munashe caught him crouching behind a bush whispering to his bazooka and caressing the long tube with the bulge in the middle. Munashe gasped, then silently turned away. He never told anybody what he had seen. And at last, when only the short man, out of the seventy of them, scored a direct hit with the lethal weapon at the shooting range during training, Munashe's puzzle unravelled. He knew that the man understood the bazooka and that he and the weapon were friends and that was when Munashe nicknamed him Bazooka and everyone started calling him by that name and the man seemed to like it. That was how they became friends.

There were many other distressing memories that Munashe had about the war; even that memorable day when he first held the AK rifle in his hands – feeling its smooth, short butt and shining brown barrel, caressing the edges of its banana-shaped magazine, tracing the cold curve of the black trigger with his forefinger – felt strangely anti-climatic. It was only after he raised the gun above his head in an effort to stir a little of his old excitement that he felt a distant pain, but one he could not identify. It was as if he had been press-ganged to join the war. Perhaps the excitement would come on the day he crossed the border back into Rhodesia to fight for the liberation of the country.

The dry Mukumbura River formed the border with Rhodesia until they reached the Mavhuradonha mountains leaving the Murenga range behind in Mozambique. Munashe felt that that stretch of the river where it twisted and turned was the reason why his long-awaited home-coming was another kind of anti-climax. Because their trail followed the river, he had the divided feeling that they were in both countries at the same time.

They followed the trail in a silent file that stretched over a kilometre and the dark night pressed hard upon them. They were seven altogether and they could not see anything, only the silhouettes of the dark mountains etched against the western night sky. Munashe looked away from the mountains and wondered whether they had at last crossed the border. Daylight found them camped up the mountain at a spot where a ridge protruded, forcing the dry, sandy river to curl again. In the morning, they went down to the dry river and dug deep in the sandy bed to extract water to quench their thirst and that reminded him of Bazooka and a sadness filled his heart.

Bazooka had died alone when the worst was almost over. For two weeks, they had wandered through heavy jungle, lost. It started with their guide falling sick from a bout of malaria; they built a stretcher-bed from bamboo poles and carried him. His condition became progressively worse and he began to give incomprehensible directions that confused them but they continued to move on, towards nowhere. Then their desperation became visible because they thought they would all die in the sun and they no longer felt the intense exhaustion, thirst and hunger, as if their minds were somehow suspended from their bodies. And that was when Bazooka, who had only talked once to Munashe during the entire journey from Chifombo, shouted hoarsely that he was being pursued by witches and ran away through the sprawling forest of heavy baobab and tangled *mopani* trees and no one followed him because no one had any strength to do so. In the silence all they heard was the crashing sound as the man ran deeper and deeper into the thick forest.

They stumbled upon his decomposing body more than a day later and saw that his arms were raised in the air as if he had died surrendering to the phantom witches that possessed his mind. His bazooka had been cast to one side, still loaded. No one, not even his friend Munashe, cried. They stood around his decomposing body in silence and none of them saw the platoon of FRELIMO soldiers arrive. It was FRELIMO who helped them to bury Bazooka and find their way again.

All the way up the steep mountain side with the sun at their backs and the snaking river below, Munashe tried to excite himself with thoughts of home and the inevitable battles that lay ahead. But all he felt was emptiness, and a peculiar remorse, and all he saw was the image of Bazooka's decomposing body sprawling across the length of his mind, and behind it the blurred image of the young woman as she bent to tie the string around his testicles, and another of himself as he stood bewildered in the middle of a crowd howling for his blood, while incredibly he confessed that he was a member of the Rhodesian Special Branch. To have admitted to something he had not done gave rise to a strange, persistent sense of shame.

At last, they got to the top of the mountain and Munashe looked down the other side and saw the land rising and falling, and the villages that clung to the sides of the land as it rose and fell, bouncing away into the horizon, and his heart beat faster as excitement stirred him at last. He peered harder into the distance, shielding his eyes from the sun with his palm, wondering whether he might not be able to make someone out. He was home.

The war began for him the following day at a temporary base on the edge of one of the villages: a surprise attack. It was carried out exactly as the Rhodesians carried out most of their military attacks: early in the morning with sleep still in everyone's eyes, when no one could quite remember where they had put their AK. That was when the first rifle shot cracked through the silence. It was a pattern that Munashe would soon know well.

He heard the noise while he stood behind one of the cattle pens passing water. What followed was like a dream. Two helicopters suddenly emerged from behind the tree tops like sinister birds of prey and began to pound their gunships at the guerrilla positions, and they returned fire in a disorderly fashion. Munashe stood stock still behind the cattle pen until he saw the section commander leap from his position, his rifle blazing on full automatic, and only then did the powerful reality of the attack strike home.

He bent down and ran towards the depression, away from the smoking village. Behind him, he could hear the voice of the section commander shouting at them to take cover and return fire. And then the two helicopters retreated and the Rhodesian ground forces, who had taken positions around the village, opened fire from the other side of the depression and Munashe knew they were completely surrounded and he thought, my god, this is war, and he began to shoot wildly, overwhelmed by the stinging smell of gunpowder while the Rhodesians kept closing in. The situation worsened while the section commander barked desperate orders at the fleeing guerrillas before he stood up and began firing from the hip. Then Munashe pulled him down, shouting at him not to behave as if he was insane, and gunfire blazed and cracked around them and there was nothing to understand.

And then the section commander shouted:

'Comrades advance!'

And Munashe noticed that the commander's voice was hoarse because something strange had happened to his mind and he tried to pull him down to the ground. Then he saw that the man had been shot through the head and in that instant the commander tumbled forward. Munashe and two other guerrillas frantically worked their way through the undergrowth and finally got to the drift still shooting wildly into the bush and then the fire from the Rhodesians died down because the smoke from the burning village made it difficult to see anything. Munashe and the other two guerrillas ran on as if they were possessed and then one of them, Gondo, calmly said that he had been shot through the shoulder and his shirt and trousers were soaked in blood.

And they saw the blood and they opened their mouths and Gondo saw it and that was when he felt the pain but Munashe was thinking about something else: the fate of his comrades and the village that had been destroyed, burnt to ash. They continued to run and a long time later Gondo cried out:

'I am dying.'

And he fell down and they took turns to carry him on their shoulders along the foot of the mountain, going east, as if they were going back to Mozambique, and in the evening they hid in a cave and waited to see what daylight would bring; Gondo cried in agony and Munashe was worried by many things. He wondered whether any other of his fellow comrades had survived the attack. He wondered if anyone from the obliterated village had survived. He could not understand how he had survived. Was this war?

Peering out through the mouth of the cave early the following morning, they saw two specks glitter against the western horizon and heard the buzzing sound and they knew they were spotter planes combing the area because the previous day's operation was not yet over. They continued to hide in the cave on the side of the mountain for several days, surviving on baobab fruit and drinking water that they had collected from a deep pool at the foot of the mountain, afraid to venture anywhere because every day the spotter planes buzzed in the sky, scouring the dry veld for victims; and behind in the dark cave, Gondo groaned in pain. This was the only noise that broke the interminable silence. Munashe spent the long, endless hours watching the animals from the adjacent Matusadonha wilderness come to the water hole, and this deferred the pain which was lingering in the background and marring the landscape.

The animals that came first were the buffalo, just after sunrise. They came to the water hole and then went to a salt-lick a short distance away. Their scabby skins were dusty brown, the colours of the African dry season. They huffed and gruffed, elbowing each other out of the way, swishing their short tails and tossing

15

their massive heads into the air to chase away the flies that swarmed around their flared nostrils and their small unpredictable yellow eyes.

Then, during the heat of the day, came the elephants, lumbering monsters that looked as if they belonged to some pre-historic period. They came in the blazing sun and walked lazily down to the water hole. Occasionally an old bull, with tusks as long as the tangled branches of the motionless *mopani* trees, would let out a sharp cry and then other members of the herd would become alert and raise their floppy ears which normally looked like wet blankets hung on a washing line to dry. After quenching their huge thirsts, they played like children, splashing about in the water, spurting it through their trunks held high like the trumpet he had played in the school band at Kutama Mission. They left one after the other, as silently as they had come, leaving behind mountains of foliage-laced dung that his mother had told him was a cure for nose-bleeding and a host of other common ailments.

The packs of howling hyenas came running just before sunset, as if, like Bazooka, they were being pursued by invisible phantoms. They hurriedly lapped the water and scampered back into the forest. Unlike the elephant and the buffalo, the hyena was a familiar animal. Munashe remembered the first time that he had seen one – in a trap set by his grandfather after these furtive, ugly animals had stolen his goats. The trap, or *chizarira*, was a tight rectangular enclosure built of heavy logs into which once the animal was shut, it could never escape. Munashe and his friends found the trapped animal, alive and howling, stuck inside it.

That was when he realized that the front legs of the hyena were longer than the hind legs which made the animal look strange; the belly hung clumsily underneath the animal as if it was valueless baggage, something forgotten at a remote rural bus stop. But it was when he was holed up in the cave on the side of the mountain that he first heard their reckless laughter as they dragged their hanging bellies into the dry, African dusk.

The lions arrived just as the sun was setting: lethal ambushes along the game trails that led to the water hole. But in all the days that he watched them, he never witnessed a kill. So he heard the lions roar angrily, as they shifted their heavy bodies around the water hole before disappearing into the night; he shivered as the two of them took turns to guard the mouth of the cave while within the dark interior, Gondo's wound grew septic, and he thought of his home and the people who, he knew, loved and missed him: his mother, father, brothers, sisters, friends, every one of them, and Munashe thought: what am I doing here? and he thought again: will I ever get out of this place alive? and he envied the animals, especially the lions, for their simple ways, and he hated himself for joining the crazy fucking war. Lions occupied a special place in his heart.

Then, one afternoon, Munashe went down the mountain to collect some water from the deep pool where the animals drank and he heard a splashing sound but because the bush around was thick, the high grass and the sun made seeing difficult. He stopped and crouched down, his heart beat faster and he began to sweat. He heard the splashing sound again. He felt afraid. And then he saw the dark mane of a lion and he released the safety-catch of his automatic rifle with a trembling hand. The lion rose from behind a thicket, his great head up, and he turned and looked at him. Their eyes met.

A long time before, when he was still at school, Munashe had learnt that if he wanted anything from his father, he asked for it by addressing the man with the family totem: Shumba, the lion. Because he was young, he did not understand why this ploy always worked. And then he began to notice that his uncles laughed

17

lightly, proudly, each time they compared themselves, they of the Shumba totem, with people of other totems. It was during such initially mystifying moments that he saw even the poorest of their totem, the ones wearing patched trousers, stand up with their heads held high – their worn, lined hands thrust deep into pockets full of holes – and brag about the exploits of the Shumba people: they were the ferocious beasts of the forest with eyes that sparked and lit veld fires, people with strong, deep voices that were kept in gourds tucked inside their throats, people who shook the ground when they moved, people of many wives: men of men. Then the lion gave a deep-throated roar which shook the ground.

He had seen lions before, from the mouth of the cave up the mountain, but he had not known the animal had such an awesome presence. As he crouched behind the bush, he saw the lion as huge, etched in the bright white afternoon sun. Then he understood the feeling of greatness that his people derived from being associated with such an animal. With its long sinuous body that thinned at the rear, a massive head, barrel-chest, heavy shoulders and smooth gilded skin, the animal watched him closely and Munashe saw the fierce light in its eyes. Then it grunted, as if in recognition, and walked majestically away. Munashe was mesmerized. The lions usually made their way to the water hole as the sun went down. What then was this one doing in the heat of the day? Was it a messenger from his ancestral spirits? He began to clap his hands and said loudly:

> *'Zvaonekwa Shumba*
> *honai ndiri ndega mumarimuka*
> *ndinokumbira kuchengetwa*
> *nokuti ini hapana chandakatadza*
> *kuuya kuhondo dzaive shungu dzenyika*
> *moturirawo vamwe venyu kumhepo ikoko.'*

The lion turned, stopped, looked back, and grunted before disappearing into the thick bush.

A tawny bateleur eagle sat silently on a dry branch at the top of the *mukamba* tree that stood next to the mouth of the cave. Munashe had only become aware of it on the second day after he had heard its sharp, forlorn shrill. It sat there motionless, looking down at them throughout the whole day. The only thing that moved were its sharp red eyes. Then, just before sunset, it took off with a sudden, powerful flap of its enormous wings that shook the trees before it sailed away into the apricot sunset. And when, early the following morning, Munashe again saw it perched silently on the dry branch of the *mukamba* tree, he thought that its nest might be somewhere nearby. And once again, it spent the whole day sitting motionless on the dry branch, looking down at them. And then it occurred to him that perhaps the bird was lonely; he felt pity for it. And when it also occurred to him that the bird might be thinking the same about them, he could not hold back the tears that filled his eyes.

'It's a bad omen,' Nyika, his companion, cried. 'We are done for!' Munashe shrugged his shoulders and looked away. Meanwhile, the stink inside the cave became unbearable: Gondo was slowly decaying alive.

Munashe left late that afternoon as the bateleur flew away – together they disappeared into the sunset. He walked all night long through the animal-infested wilderness towards the village which now seemed a long way away. He walked like an automaton, only vaguely hearing the proliferation of sounds in the dark bush which surrounded him; not the reckless howl of the hyena, nor the sharp, disjointed cough of the leopard, not the high-pitched shrill from the hill to the east, nor the ceaseless chorus of a multitude of screeching insects. What he heard was the beating of the gigantic wings of the bateleur as it took off from the *mukamba* tree and sailed into the night, the deep-throated grunt of the lion and the wailing voices of people at a funeral: these sounds filled his head.

He reached the first village early the following morning and knocked on the door of the first hut. By the time an old man came out to answer his knock, Munashe felt ready to collapse from exhaustion, hunger and thirst. And by the time the rescue team from the village reached the cave on the mountainside early in the morning of the following day, Gondo was already dead. Slowly they sealed the mouth of the cave with stones and left.

Halfway down the rocky slope, Munashe stopped and looked back up at the huge *mukamba* tree and saw the tawny bateleur eagle sitting on a dry branch, holding a guinea-fowl in its strong talons. And then bewilderingly the bird released the guinea-fowl from its grip and it fell down at the mouth of the cave. An elder villager in the team saw it. He also saw the bateleur eagle lift off with a ferocious flap of its wide wings, emitting a piercing shrill, and Munashe saw its eyes flash fiercely in the sun and the old villager said:

'The bird is the guardian spirit of the mountain. You were protected.' And he went and crouched and clapped his hands before picking up the guinea-fowl. And the great bird rose higher and higher into the cloudless sky until it became a black dot in the blue air. Munashe strained his eyes to keep it in view but at last it slipped beyond sight into the vast shimmering horizon. And it was then that the villagers told them that one of their colleagues had survived the attack and was waiting to be reunited with the group and that the bodies of the three guerrillas who had been killed had been airlifted and stuffed in polythene containers that were dangled beneath the belly of a helicopter which had twice circled the entire district before it flew towards Mount Darwin, more than a hundred kilometres to the south.

But the villagers did not mention that fifteen of their fellow tribesmen had been killed and that headman Kajese's village had been burnt to the ground.

Then the three of them huddled together at the edge of the village like abandoned chickens and wondered what to do, and Nyika said:

'Let's go back to the rear.'

And Hodo, for that was the name of the third comrade, said:

'That is the only thing we can do.'

And they both looked at Munashe and he shrugged his shoulders because his mind was fixed on something else, a bateleur soaring high over the roof of his mind and the words of the old villager:

'It's the guardian spirit of the mountain. You were protected.'

So that Nyika asked:

'What do you think, Comrade Munashe?'

Munashe waved his hand unconsciously and said nothing. And it was the old villager who was standing nearby who came to his rescue.

'There is a group of comrades operating across the Ruya River. I can take you there.'

And he took them there, three walking days away. The old villager handed them over to a section commander who had a pleasant personality and Munashe could not understand how there could be such commanders in the war. It was beyond all his experience of life in the struggle since touching down from Botswana at Lusaka international airport: the short journey in the Land Rover, the security chief with inflamed eyes behind the wheel; the young female security officer who tied a string around his testicles; the vicious commanders in training whom he had watched work on Bazooka until the poor chap was no longer certain that he was not a witch; the tough guide from Chifombo

21

across the Zambezi River who warned them that they would drink their urine when their water reserves were used up, and whose eyes lit up with delight when he saw the astonishment in their eyes, that is until malaria brought him down; the tough section commander shooting wildly from the hip during the surprise attack until he succumbed to enemy fire. Indeed the war seemed congested with commanders with the capacity to hold life in their open palms and stare down at it. And the section commander even liked him! He could not understand it.

So that when the field detachment commander came a few weeks later to get the details about how more than half a section could be wiped out in a single attack without either the villagers, or any of the guerrillas, selling out to the enemy, it was the section commander who immediately came to their defence and said that such things happened in war. The detachment commander had kept quiet but it was evident from the way he cast his eyes down that he was not wholly satisfied. And it was when he wanted to deploy the three who had survived the catastrophic attack into various sections operating further inland that the section commander requested that Munashe be allowed to remain in his section: the detachment commander's face had clouded but he had nevertheless agreed to it.

And it was then that the war changed for Munashe and he did not know whether to believe it or not; it seemed like a dream. All he could feel was the excitement growing inside his chest, making his fingers itch. He had not realized that the villagers had stopped singing and that Tonderayi, the section commander, was delivering the *pungwe's* political lesson. So that when he finally heard the section commander talking about the civilizations that existed in the country before the coming of the white man, he was shocked to discover that the history of his people did not start with the coming of the whites. The section commander began

22

with the Munhumutapa and the Rozvi empires during the Great Zimbabwe civilization, and continued on to the coming of the white man and the first *chimurenga*, and on through the various forms of colonial government up to Ian Smith's UDI, when the last bridge between blacks and whites was burned down and the only way left to communicate was through violence: the war, the second *chimurenga*.

Then the section commander stopped and burst into song and the villagers stoked it up with their voices and the flames leapt into the night, evoking the memories of the heroes of the first *chimurenga*. Munashe listened to it all, a short distance behind the section commander. It was when he heard the refrain about their blood mingling with that of the living that he felt the numbness in his head. So that by the time it reached the dance, he could see the young woman carrying a baby on her back at the edge of the semi-circle wait impatiently to snatch the song away from Tonderayi and run away with it. And when at last she succeeded, she blazed a crackling trail and everyone followed her, as if she was pursuing the fleeing spirits of the long-gone heroes so that they would all become one with them. And when they lost the song and the spirits in the thickets where she had led them, then the dancing to the fury of the drum began.

The bare feet of the villagers hit the ground wildly and churned up dust that swathed them, while all Munashe could hear was the fury of the thudding drum. It carved its own trail, away from the thicket where they had lost the song, and Munashe caught a flashing glimpse of the drummer. He was an old man with a long white beard that shone in the moonlight, his furrowed face averted towards the sky while his hands worked fiercely on the drum.

And when at last the song was found and returned to the young woman with the baby on her back by a small boy herding cattle in the veld, when the drummer and his drum were finally reunited, when the young woman with the baby on her back gave the song back to the section commander, Munashe moved away from the crowd and stood alone behind a hut and wept. He had not known it was possible to feel and become so at one with the war. And he wished that an opportunity would arise that would enable him to tell the section commander his story; to tell him how disillusioned he had become and how he had blamed himself for joining the struggle; and to perhaps have the chance to listen to the section commander tell his own story; how he had acquired the glint in his eyes; where he had got the spring in his step; how he had lent metal to his voice. But all they did was move on with the wind and the moon at their backs, never sleeping in one place more than once, crossing and re-crossing the Ruya River, sighting but avoiding the enemy, only laying anti-tank mines on the main roads to Rushinga, Karanda and Dotito during the night, and then observing them from the surrounding hills during the day: billowing dust mushrooming in the sky as the fatal detonation occurred, the booming sound following a long while afterwards. The sound always came such a long time later, that the opportunity to tell his story to the section commander never occurred.

Then one night, the detachment commander came and took the section commander aside and Munashe watched him as he talked in a frenzied voice, making gestures with his hands, pointing towards the mountains across the border; and the section commander listened impassively, without making any movement save to nod his head occasionally. And then the detachment commander called aside the section security commander and talked to him in a hushed voice, and then they both threw furtive glances at the section commander; and when at last the detachment commander disappeared into the night, the section security commander went and talked briefly with the section commander and the following day, Munashe noticed that his eyes had lost their shine; that there was a perceptible drag in his step and that the metal in his voice had lost its smoothness. He also noticed the section security commander watched the section commander all the time, following him wherever he went, even to relieve himself behind the bushes, and he knew that he would never be able to tell him the story of his life because something was seriously wrong.

And yet three days later as they trekked back to Mozambique, for that was the instruction that the detachment commander had left them, the section commander stopped and looked at him and said:

'The night the villagers brought you over from the mountain, I mistook you for one of my former students at Highfield Community School in Salisbury. His name was Andrew and he was brilliant. I spent the night seething with anger, waiting for a confrontation with him the following morning. I wanted to ask him just one question but fortunately it turned out that it wasn't him but you and I kept the question to myself. And then it turned out that I liked you and ever since I have been fighting back the same question and now I can't keep it in any more: Why did you join this war?'

'I don't understand.'

'You don't understand?' he asked angrily.

Munashe started because he had never heard the section commander sound so angry and he raised his hand defensively and the section commander noticing the gesture said:

'Damn it. I know you have been through high school, perhaps even university, and this is what makes me angry. This war does not have the capacity to utilize people like you. It will, instead, destroy you. It is so different from what we day-dreamed about back in Salisbury. Damn it boy, there is no honour in more than

25

half the things that are done here, all in the name of the war.' He glanced over his shoulder, at the security officer hovering close by.

And Munashe gasped because he had not realized the section commander was moving around in huge circles, chipping small pieces off the story of his own life. What exactly was he driving at?

'Damn you man, why don't you ask me why I joined the war?' he asked and quickly turned aside but Munashe had already seen the tears in his eyes.

Father Erasmus rubbed the tears away from his eyes and looked at them. The priest talked about freedom with a passion that Munashe, and indeed every other boy, thought of as peculiar. The Irish priest cried each time he talked about freedom during their weekly lesson that he called civics. His lips trembled and his eyes burned as he equated freedom with love:

'I may speak with the tongues of men and angels but if I am not a free man, I am as hollow as an echoing gong,' he said, slightly twisting Saint Paul's emotional letter to the Corinthians.

He continued: 'I may have the power to foretell events and to understand all mysteries but if I am not free, I am nothing.' The boys continued to clap their hands and the priest's eyes burned more fiercely. 'I may give all my worldly possessions to the poor and surrender my body to be sacrificed for their cause but if both myself and they are not free, my gestures would be futile because it is freedom that gives value to our actions. Freedom is the embodiment of all our hopes, dreams and aspirations.' He paused and looked at them and then continued:

'When I was a child, the most important lesson that I was taught was respect for other people but it was only when I grew up that I realized that one could not possibly respect others when one did not acknowledge their freedom. There is no respect in a

26

situation of bondage. And so it can be said that of all the gifts that God gave us, there is none as great as freedom. Therefore, the worst sin that any man can commit is to deny another this God-given gift.'

Munashe heard himself shout: 'But that's what's happening to us in this country, Father!' He looked around at the others: 'Is that not so, guys?' he pleaded and they nodded their heads and the old priest looked away and lit his pipe and stared thoughtfully out through the window and then rubbed his hands together.

'I am merely talking about theology that liberates the spirit. What you might have understood me to mean is purely conjectural.'

And Munashe sat down because the Angelus began to ring and the priest led them to say the mid-day Hail Mary and they responded 'Full of grace' and thus another civics lesson ended. And so it was that the priest, who was also the principal, suddenly disappeared from the mission and the boys did not know where he had gone because nobody ever told them until at last they heard that the man had been deported from the country. The senior boys planned a demonstration: poorly organized, it was badly attended and the police took away the alleged ring leaders and they were never seen at the school again; but for Munashe the world had changed forever.

So that when he was in his final year at the school, he wrote a controversial play, *Battle Front*, to highlight the plight of the Tangwena people who were then being evicted from their ancestral land by the government. Their predicament conjured painful memories of the evictions of his own childhood. His intention was to stage the play throughout the country and give the proceeds to the chief to help him pay the legal costs of the court battles but the school authorities advised against it because they knew the play would infuriate the government. And it was at this time when Munashe's spirits were at their lowest ebb that he got the letter from the priest in Ireland:

Child,

What I find most intriguing about Battle Front *is you, yourself. I clearly remember the day when, on impulse, you stood up and pleaded with everyone in the class to do something positive about the plight of your people.*

Now your play has taken you a step beyond that plea. It is a call to everyone to declare their position in the conflict that will inevitably embroil your people and your country.

Remember, freedom is God-given. The most honourable fight in which one can engage is the active pursuit of freedom. So one day, when you are a man among free people, those of you – alive or dead – who were involved in the fight for freedom, will stand to be acknowledged as the heroes of your struggle. And I shall be there to witness that occasion.

Yours in Christ

Fr. V. Erasmus SJ.

When he had finished reading the letter, he buried it at the bottom of his suitcase where it remained until he abandoned his university studies to join the war.

'So you were a teacher?'

The section commander did not answer. He only shrugged his shoulders and moved on, mumbling something about misplaced commitments and dashed dreams. Munashe shook his head and followed him. The security officer moved in close behind them.

'Someone help me, please!' Munashe cried, looking down at the hoe with the broken handle at his feet. The security officer let out another burst of automatic fire into the sky and the female combatant shouted:

'He is wasting time, *chef*.'

And somehow that incensed the security officer who grabbed the hoe and shoved it into Munashe's hands howling that if he did not go ahead and finish off the woman and her baby that would leave him with no choice but to shoot him as he had the other three rebels whose grave was behind the baobab tree. Munashe held the hoe in his hands and looked at the woman but he did not see her. He only vaguely heard the sound of the crying baby. He knew that the woman was looking at him through her swollen eyes. He also knew that the base commander was behind him, his head averted.

'Are we going to stand here the whole day waiting for the coward to make up his mind whether to perform the execution or not? God! There are more important things to do. The war is not over yet.'

'But does it have to be a hoe?' the base commander argued again.

'Shut up, rebel sympathizer!' screamed the security officer, pointing his rifle at the base commander.

The base commander helplessly shook his head and walked away. Behind him, he could hear the vicious cracks as someone hit Munashe again and again and his shredded voice as he asked to be forgiven for being a coward, telling them he had never done such a thing before and the female combatant retorting that no one had begged him to join the war, and the condemned woman watching everything through her swollen eyes, gently rocking the baby crying on her back and waiting patiently for her fate.

Then Munashe tightened his grip around the broken hoe handle and whispered something to himself that he did not know and tears and sweat rolled down his face. And all the while, he

29

looked away from the woman as if he was afraid that she might ask him to forgive her. He could also hear, above the noise of the crying baby, her faint, agonized breathing and he saw that she was shaking. He held the hoe firmly in both hands and its steel gleamed eerily in the sun.

'I can't do it!' a scream broke from Munashe.

'Can he not use the gun?' the base commander implored.

'Shut up!'

'Go on! Strike the fatal blow!' someone yelled but Munashe did not know who it was because he was tightening his grip around the raised, broken handle and he kept whispering something to himself, something that he did not know because somewhere in his mind he feared that the woman might ask him why he was about to do what he was about to do and he would not be able to give her any answer at all because he did not know what the talked-about revolt was all about. He knew that he was merely caught up in it, like so many other things in the war, such as his weird confession that he was an enemy agent and Bazooka's confession that he was a witch, and the section commander to whom he could now never tell his story because he had been taken away, and the baby continued to cry. Then he looked at the haggard figure of the woman and it lost its shape and its edges got torn and the baby on her back became a protrusion of her hunched back and then he swung the hoe, and he heard the blade swishing furiously through the air and he thought of the sound from the enormous wings of the bateleur as it took off from the towering *mukamba* tree at the mouth of the cave on the side of the mountain and the foul smell from the inside as Gondo groaned, decaying, dying. The war was an insatiable incinerator that would burn them all up, one after the other.

The woman fell down with the first vicious blow and the sound of Munashe's jarred and violent cry mingled with that of the dying baby as the hoe fell again and again and again until Munashe was splattered all over with dark brown blood and the base commander held him back and he refused, shouting that he wished that someone had killed him because he could not live with such a memory and the security officer pulled the base commander away, threatening that he would personally deal with him now that the wife and child of one of Badza's chief lieutenants had been taken care of. Then Munashe threw away the blood-smeared hoe and walked away blindly, past the huge baobab, past the earth mound where the other three rebels had been hastily buried, towards nowhere. All he could hear were the last cries of the baby as it died. Strangely, there was no trace of any smell of blood at all. He could not understand it, nor why it took the baby so long to die. Nightmare and war became interchangeable.

So that when he was finally sent back to the front as part of the new-look Chimanda detachment operating between the Mazoe River and the Ruya River, he moved in a dazed way, seeing the things around him as if they were very far away and feeling as if they were not part of him, being there but not feeling there, just moving on, numbed to the news of the death of party supremo and chairman of the War Council, Herbert Chitepo, in a car bomb in Lusaka, never giving a second thought to the news of the subsequent arrest of the entire military High Command, paying no attention to the news of the release of all the nationalist leaders in Salisbury; he was just moving on.

But slowly he became aware of the heightened enemy patrols, making it difficult for them to sleep and rest. Then their most effective armament, the anti-tanks, ran out. The detachment commander quickly dispatched the section that operated along the Ruya River back to the rear for replenishment. And behind, they waited and waited and waited, shifting from one base to another, and sometimes to a third within one day, hoping that once the section from the rear returned with the consignment of anti-tank mines, they would use them to control the rampant progress of the Rhodesians, but the section did not return.

Then one morning, Munashe saw a spotter plane circling in the sky, a voice shouting through loud-speakers that the war was over, that they should lay down their arms and surrender at the nearest army or police camp or for that matter at any district administrative office; shouting that their leaders recently released from prison were engaged in negotiations with the government; shouting that they had renounced terrorism and what remained was to work out how they could be accommodated in government because independence had at last come to the country. The message from the loud-speakers ended by labelling those who did not comply with the directive as terrorists and threatened that they would face the wrath of the Rhodesian security forces. And Munashe saw the plane drop leaflets carrying the same message, so the sky became white with floating paper and the villagers dubbed it the day that the sky rained paper and there was confusion within the ranks of the guerrillas because a lot of things that they did not understand were happening and the detachment commander moved from one section to the other telling them that their orders came from Zambia and not from the sky but he knew, just as they did, that the High Command had been imprisoned and that fresh arms supplies were not coming and that the only thing to understand was that the Rhodesians were everywhere, hot on their battered, weary trail.

And then the situation became so bad that the detachment commander took four fighters, two from Munashe's section and two from the other, and said he personally was going back to Terçeira to find out why the section he had sent to bring in fresh arms supplies had not returned and whether it was true that the entire High Command had been arrested and imprisoned and if so for what reason and to establish whether it was true that the war had ended and if that was the case why they, at the front, had not been informed through the normal channels and finally to find out what sort of a ceasefire or truce it was that required them to lay down their arms and surrender to the Rhodesians as if they had lost the war. But four days later, two villagers came and told them that the detachment commander had been ambushed as he attempted to cross the Ruya River and all the five of them had perished in the attack. And that day, the rains fell.

For a whole week, it had continued: an enormous dark cloud came in low from the western sky late in the afternoon, labouring towards the east but then a gust of driving wind came howling through the dry land, breaking and scattering the bewildered cloud, leaving the barren countryside enveloped in a thick blanket of swirling dust. But on the day that the two villagers brought news of the death of the detachment commander and his four colleagues, the dark cloud hovered over the mountain to the east, then gathering its heavy grey strength it descended in a heavy downpour. It rained the whole night, the following day and the day after that and the guerrillas breathed a sigh of relief because they knew that the Rhodesians would not travel in such lashing rain and that new vegetation would soon clothe the countryside and provide the guerrillas with cover and for the first time in a long time, they slept at one place and rested their aching muscles. And Munashe moved about in the rain, mumbling that *mvura ishamwari yangu*, opening his palms to try and hold the downpour, behaving as if he were insane.

Indeed *mbanje* had already intruded into their ugly life in the desperate war. They smoked it in the morning and in the after-

33

noon and in the evening and just before they trudged on during the night as they changed bases. It raised their spirits and it was the only thing, Munashe realized, that reassured him that he could after all survive the routine killings, the unabated savagery and the dying. And it had a special, almost mystical healing effect: he could literally decide what he wanted to think about, what he wanted to dream about, what he wanted to be, what he wanted to happen. During those moments, the war was suddenly over and he was back in Salisbury, taking in breathfuls of the city air that he could smell laced with burning oil from the belching factories, and he could hear the rumbling metallic roar as the city surged forward and he could see the explosion of colours in Rufaro Stadium on a Sunday afternoon during a crucial soccer match between the city arch-rivals, Dynamos and Chibuku Shumba. And once in a while, he would ask Lillian, his childhood sweetheart, to accompany him as he went window-shopping along the First Street Mall. *Mbanje* provided him with the chance to escape from the brutal war and its ruthless experiences, to dream as he wanted, to be where he wanted, and even to stay there, and the others saw it and they worried about him. Then the section commander took him aside and said:

'No one knows how this fighting will end, or when this war will be over, but we should not lose hope because we all wish for independence and to be welcomed home as heroes.'

Munashe remained silent, thinking about what the section commander had said. What shook him was that in all his fantasies, he had never dreamt of the war reaching an end, he had never dreamt of independence. He had not wanted to spoil his dreams of home with thoughts of the war, or its outcome. When he had arrived at Lusaka airport, had the security chief with the flaming eyes talked about the end of the war, he would have felt elated, even honoured, at the thought of contributing

34

something, no matter how small, towards independence: but not now. There was nothing in the war nor how it was prosecuted for people like him. All he wanted was to be left alone, to be allowed the chance to dream and then like all the others, including the woman with the crying baby on her back, his death would come: it was inevitable. He shook his head and walked away. The section commander stared at his hunched receding figure and shrugged his shoulders.

And because the rains had temporarily stopped, the Rhodesians resumed their counter-offensive and Munashe's section commander arranged to meet the commander of another section to decide what to do in the face of confusion as they were operating in isolation with nothing coming from the rear and it was agreed that they should all return to the main base in Mozambique but intelligence information they received from the villagers indicated that the Rhodesians had massed themselves along the border, rendering any such attempt suicidal, and the only wise option left to them was to stay holed up inside the country until, as Munashe put it bluntly, it was their turn to die.

Then one afternoon as they camped on a small hill straddling the dividing line between Chimhanda and Rusambo districts, a thin guerrilla whom they called Sly walked up to him and sat down beside him and stared into the white blanket of falling rain. Munashe wiped away the water trickling into his eyes and barely glanced at him. Company made him feel crowded. He wanted to be left alone to dream.

'I don't like the rain,' Sly said in a depressed voice. Munashe did not answer.

'They say the Rhodesians have sealed the border,' he continued. Munashe kept his face averted and said nothing. Sly looked down at the AK with a folding butt on his lap. 'Shit!' he cursed. 'What exactly is going on? Is there still anyone out at the rear? If there is, why have they abandoned us? What are we supposed to do?'

Munashe continued to stare at the rain although he did not see it. He only felt the anger. He wanted to be left alone.

'And this news that all the nationalists have been released from prison and are in Lusaka, is it true? When will this war end?'

'Please leave me alone!'

'All I want is a chance to see my mother and father again. Is that asking for too much of this fucking war?'

Munashe turned and looked at the thin bedraggled guerrilla. 'Moaning will not help end the war. We're in it and that's that. Who did not leave a mother and a father behind? Some even left wives and children!'

'I am tired of the shit war. I am tired of not knowing what will happen to me tomorrow. I am tired of waiting to die. I am tired of the endless killings. I am tired of everything.'

'SHUT UP!'

'If you have forgotten *Mudhara* Kachidza at Bveke village, I haven't. I cannot forget that incident.'

Mudhara Kachidza's case was just another example of brutality in a brutal war. It happened when their ammunition reserves had dwindled to a precarious level and so the Rhodesians, sensing victory, intensified their offensive. Indeed their entire section would have perished if one of the girls who had brought their food had not whispered that it had been poisoned. But she was not fast enough to save Paradzai and Zex. The two died the following day, reducing the section to six because Sly, the section political commissar, had not yet deserted. Munashe watched in horror as the poisoned men changed colour whilst they writhed in agony. By the time they died, they had turned green.

Many, many years later as he walked along the street in Mutare, he came upon a man who had been knocked down in a car accident and because the police had not yet arrived, his mangled, twisted body lay uncovered in the middle of the road. When he looked closer, he thought the dead man looked green and the incident brought back violent memories of the painful deaths of his colleagues and there was fear in his eyes as he blindly walked away, bumping into bewildered people who had gathered around the victim.

And the guerrillas' subsequent investigations into the food-poisoning led them to *Mudhara* Kachidza's door-step. They went to his home late the following night but somehow the man had got wind of their arrival and had fled. They rounded up his three wives and thirteen children. They threatened to kill them unless they disclosed where the man of the family was and one of the wives told them that he had fled to the army camp at Rushinga for protection and the section commander immediately dispatched Sly and two other guerrillas in pursuit. About two hours later, they brought *Mudhara* Kachidza back, his hands tied behind him. He shook as he led them to the place where he had hidden not only the bottle of poison but also a two-way radio communication set and a carton of batteries. And then the guerrillas became paranoid with rage and hit him with both their fists and boots and the old man cried, saying he had been tempted by money, and someone asked him how much and he said he still had not been given the initial one hundred dollars of the promised five thousand and the guerrillas went berserk hitting everything in their way and someone let out a burst of automatic fire and the section commander said shit! because he knew the noise would surely attract the Rhodesians and there was nothing to understand.

Munashe sneaked away behind the fowl-run in the village and listened to the pandemonium. And when at last he caught whiffs of paraffin in the damp night air, he knew the horrible routine had started. And he moved further away from the painful confusion because, already, he could hear the plaintive cry of the baby ahead of the doomed crying of the old man torched and flaming.

'I set the old man alight!' Sly said, fidgeting with the gun on his lap.

'So what?' Munashe said mercilessly. 'Who hasn't done that?'

'God, I can't bear it any more. I still want to live.'

Standing, Munashe looked down at him sceptically. 'Don't tell me you are taking those messages from the sky seriously!'

'How do you know the others aren't doing the same?'

'I wouldn't do it.'

'I have never told you this before,' he looked furtively over his shoulder at the others through the falling rain. 'My father was a driver for Lever Brothers in Salisbury and we stayed in Kambuzuma.' He paused as if he was reluctant to continue. 'When this nightmare is over and you happen to be in Rufaro Stadium where everyone will be celebrating their victory, I shall be there, tucked somewhere at the back of the cheering crowd on the Eastern Grand Stand. And if you happen to look my way and our eyes meet, what you think of me is your own damn business. Nothing can any longer shame me. My friend, I am not a hero and I don't want to be one. I am just a poor ordinary person who wants to live.'

He disappeared with his gun that night and there was unusual silence in the section the following day, as if all of a sudden, each one of them was wrestling with a problem that was so personal it could not be shared with anyone else. It was as if Sly's desertion had exposed them to their own individual vulnerabilities, and how defenceless they all were. And then the section commander walked over to Munashe and sat down heavily beside him.

'He talked to you about it, didn't he?'

Munashe was silent.

'I am not trying to blame his desertion on you but they will kill him. The bastard didn't know that, did he?'

'He said he would be there, a member of the intoxicated crowd in Rufaro Stadium on the day we celebrate independence.'

The section commander burst out laughing. 'I wish I could see it that way.' He paused and then said: 'Did he say when that would be?'

Munashe shrugged his shoulders and looked away.

Unlike other desertions which caused fear, panic and bitterness among those left behind, Sly's departure was almost a non-event apart from the nagging anxiety and restlessness it created. He had nothing to take to the Rhodesians; no secret operational information and battle plans because they no longer carried out deliberate military operations, no secret information about hidden arms caches because they had depleted their reserves and had not received any fresh supplies, no secret information about guerrilla reinforcements from the rear because they had no idea what was going on there. Sly had no more than his assault rifle with a folding butt and fully charged magazine and his disillusionment with the war.

Less than a week later, they got information about him from their village intelligence network: the poor man had not surrendered at the nearest army camp as they had presumed. He had instead hidden his gun and attempted to sneak out of the operational area, perhaps to board a bus to the city where he would be reunited with his parents but he had not made it. The Rhodesians had caught him and he had led them to the spot where he had hidden his weapon and from that point, the truth about what had really happened to him became blurred. One version was that they had shot him and dumped his body in a disused mineshaft. The other was that he was taken to Rushinga blindfolded and then to Bindura where he was awaiting trial for various offences under the Law and Order Maintenance Act. And they all quickly forgot him, all that is except Munashe. Munashe thought about him every day, wondering how the poor man ever imagined he could make his way to Salisbury and slip quietly back into civilian life without being noticed. Was that the level of disorientation that they had reached? he asked himself and shook his head and waited.

And then one cloudy afternoon as they lay in the thick undergrowth at the foot of a small hill a short distance away from the Mazoe River, a young boy from the village ran breathlessly up to them and told them that six South African commandos with sniffer dogs were bathing down by the river and Munashe suggested that they go down there but the section commander warned against making any move that might compromise their already dangerous position. But Munashe insisted, saying that death was already shadowing them wherever they went and that it was only a question of time as to when it would seize them and the section commander eventually succumbed and they went down to the river under the thick cover of the undergrowth with Munashe leading the straggling file of five. As suddenly as a violent clap of thunder, he felt all the anger bottled up inside him.

He felt overwhelmed with anger about the killing, the suffering and the desolation, the desperation, the loneliness and the endless pain; he felt angry, angry about the war. But what made him almost blindingly angry was that he had allowed himself to be involved in a war where the only prospect on hand was death and the infliction of death on others. And then he thought of Sly and once again, he realized how helpless they all were.

'It's all bullshit, that message from the sky: bullshit. They will kill you once they lay their hands on you,' he said the day before the night of Sly's desertion.

'Kill me?' Sly had retorted. 'There is nothing left for them to kill. I died a long time ago. How could I not know that and live?'

His words became his epitaph.

And Munashe was to use them.

So that as he led the way along the dark meandering river, which reminded him of a writhing mamba, its head reared, he wished their file was like a mamba, its head raised, poised for the fatal strike. He was the lethal head of the black snake, its forked tongue flicking, its unblinking eyes sitting high on its forehead staring fearlessly ahead. He felt like an enraged mamba callous with recoiled anger, ready to kill what he never ate. He felt cold-blooded and ruthless. He no longer had a self. He was the war. And then he fleetingly perceived a movement and he knew that it was the commandos and he signalled the man behind him to stop.

It was the sniffer dogs that gave the guerrillas away but the commandos did not have time to scramble out of the water and reach their FN assault rifles that lay strewn on the edge of the sprawling pool. The baying dogs pounced and the guerrillas released a hail of automatic fire but, as Munashe later admitted, the dogs gave them a real scare. Then there was a horrible fire-fight but the commandos had little chance. They were quickly subdued: three were killed and the other three captured and then Munashe went berserk. He flicked open the bayonet on the end of his rifle and screaming, charged at one of the commandos. The others looked on in disbelief. He lanced the commando through the heart and the South African soldier bellowed, raising his hands in the air. Munashe pulled out the bayonet dripping blood and then thrust it in again and again and again shouting words that no one understood until the section commander rushed forward asking what he thought he was bloody doing and he held him back and the naked body of the dying commando

41

convulsed as it slumped forward. And Munashe made one last defiant effort to lunge at the dying commando but the section commander held him back.

'We have a code of military operational ethics! Had he not surrendered?'

'Had Sly not surrendered?' Munashe retorted angrily.

'You are right, sir. The Geneva Convention clearly . . .' shouted one of the two remaining commandos but his words were cut short.

'Fuck your Geneva Convention!' Munashe snarled and let out a burst of fire that tore through the commando's face and split his skull open.

The section commander hit him viciously across the face with his clenched fist and Munashe staggered, before tumbling down to the ground. He rose up dazed and cursing and walked away. But for the first time since Sly deserted, he felt cleansed. It was as if the savage killings had exorcised his anger. He walked down the river whistling a tune that he did not know he still remembered. The words of the song went:

> Vanaamai muchasara mega
> vanababa muchasara mega
> nokuti pfungwa dzangu
> dzafunga kure

It told the story of a young man wishing good-bye to his mother and father because he was going on a long journey to a far country. The young man never returns because death meets him on his way.

Behind him, Munashe heard one single gunshot ring out and he knew what they had done to the last commando. Instead of the usual plaintive cry of the baby somewhere in his mind and the air exploding with the biting smell of gunpowder, he was flooded with the sickening smell of warm, fresh blood and it reminded him of all those Christmases long ago when his father slaughtered a beast for the occasion.

He dreaded Christmas because of the smell of blood. The slaughterhouse was a flat rock behind the cattle-pen and each time he saw a tethered ox being led to it, he had cried a little inside. His father and the other village boys called him a coward because he could not stand the slow arching swing of the axe aimed somewhere between the ears of the animal, the fatal piercing crack and the doomed bellow of the ox as it slumped to the ground. And just as quickly, the sharp blade of his father's enormous hunting knife would gleam in the sun as another old man slashed the throat of the convulsing beast and, holding a container below the neck with his other hand, collected the blood that gushed out like water from a fountain. That was when Munashe knew blood had its own peculiar smell: the smell of death.

So he would not wait for any more of the sight and the smell that harrowed and sickened him. And then much later, when they eventually got round to eating the boiled blood mixed with herbs that his father said could only be eaten by men to enhance their virility, he watched from a distance, eager, like every village boy, to strengthen his virility because he wanted to be a man but knowing that if he went any closer, the smell of blood would make him want to throw up. He dreaded Christmas beause of the smell of blood.

Munashe married a few long years after the war ended and his new wife's first problem was her husband's nightmares: the tearing screams and drenching sweat.

'The night becomes a window into his life during the war,' she once told her mother.

The woman remained silent.

'One night he is ambushed and he screams at his fellow comrades to take cover and return fire. On another he is pleading with his comrades not to kill an informer. Sometimes he is at Nyadzonia talking to his fellow comrades as they bury their dead. His dreams are all about killing and dying. The night is the most dreadful time for both of us. It's as if the war had begun all over again.'

'Do you ever talk to him about the war?' her mother asked.

The nightmare still with him, Munashe raised his body from the floor, where chased by soldiers he had thrown himself. 'I don't want to think about the war but I am pursued by ghosts. They will not let me go.'

'Did you know that sometimes you hold me protectively during your bad dreams, and refuse to do what the ghosts demand that you do?'

Munashe looked at her as if he wanted to say something, and then walked to the door but she stopped him.

'Why is it that you never talked about ordinary things, with the other guerrillas? Were there no moments of light relief?'

Munashe turned and looked at her and said: 'The war was a violent time when people thought about nothing else except killing or being killed. There were no real people in the war. We were automatons. I don't know whether you understand what I'm saying because I can't make it any simpler,' and he walked out into the afternoon Sakubva sun.

From outside, Sakubva township looked desolate. It had the colour of poverty, a morbid grey. Ever since he had begun living there a few years previously, Munashe had noticed the painful degree of disinterest the township seemed to have in itself: a depressing sense of resignation. It was dirty and overcrowded. There was an air of stagnation about it, as if its clock never moved beyond the forties when the township was built: communal toilets, communal bathrooms, communal water-taps and the dust-swathed bougainvillea hedges that surrounded the squalid, drum-shaped houses. Dust billowed up from the untarred roads in blinding eddies and settled on the curved roofs, the grey walls, the windows and their broken panes and, together with that already collected on the hedges, gave Sakubva its colour.

The women of the township went about their business in a detached way as if they did not bother about tomorrow. The children played in the sludge of the township's constantly blocked drainage system. The men went to work and came back home to dream about changed fortunes in times to come. Munashe saw all this and wondered how his dead comrades would feel about such a hopeless situation, having paid with their lives for change.

Because Mutare, and Sakubva, one of its high-density suburbs, were snuggled between mountains, the night came quickly and the surrounding hills turned into a bluish floating haze. A heavy shadow descended and flooded the town leaving it dark and cold. The western sky flamed, tinged with a coat of gold, and the town curled up and slept but Munashe did not see any of this. He was frightened of the night because it was then that for him the war began all over again. His wife looked out through the window at the night sky and sighed.

'Why don't you leave him?' her mother suggested. 'The life that you are leading with him is not a life. It's Munashe, not you, that went out to fight and did whatever he did. Besides, you are still young.'

'I can't leave him, Mother.'

'Why?'

'I have to help him. He is my husband.'

'But you are not his people! How can you help him?'

'Each time I suggest that we should visit his family in Mhondoro to discuss the problem, he refuses to go. He thinks the memories will disappear on their own. But I think they have got worse.'

'My fear is that one night he will kill you and blame it on the ghosts of war.'

'I wish you understood that it's much more complicated than that. Mysterious things have happened to him.'

'What do you mean?'

'I don't quite remember you,' Munashe replied, scrutinizing the man.

'It's such a long time ago anyway,' he said, glancing away. Munashe felt there was something familiar about those eyes with their bruised look, as if they saw beyond this world. He had met the man by accident on the path between Musami Mission and the village to the east on an anxious journey to see his uncle in an attempt to prove to himself that there was nothing wrong with him.

'Yes, it's such a long, long time ago,' the man said in a sad, detached voice and suddenly Munashe remembered who he was – the Rhodesian rifleman in the battle of Bopoma River, near Marymount Mission, two weeks after his section had massacred the South African commandos. They had thrown themselves into this battle in a desperate attempt to break through the multiple Rhodesian lines and cross the border into Mozambique.

It had been a difficult decision to make but they had all realized that if they remained holed up in the country as they had initially planned to do, they would eventually be captured or killed. The section commanders of the two remaining sections of the Chimanda detachment had got them together and sub-divided them into four small units of three. The four units had then simultaneously attacked four Rhodesian operational bases strung out between the Mazoe River in the south and Mukosa School, about sixty kilometres to the north. Their idea was to create confusion

46

among the Rhodesians so that at least some of the guerrillas might slip through the lines and cross the border. Munashe's small unit, of which he was the commander, was assigned to attack the Rhodesian base at Marymount Mission. It was an almost impossible venture. A long time later as they wasted away, disarmed, guarded by FRELIMO, at Tembwe in Mozambique during what was dubbed détente, Munashe would joke about the promotion he was given at Marymount as something essentially worthless because they knew he would not live long enough to enjoy it.

The attack, under the cover of darkness, had indeed taken the Rhodesians by surprise but those who were in positions outside the camp immediately returned fire, and the night was lit by searchlights and trailers from tracer bullets. Munashe shouted ceasefire! and the guerrillas clutched their weapons and ran through the mission grounds, past the hospital, over the football pitch, towards the small hill that formed an eerie silhouette against the eastern sky. There was gunfire from the hill and they quickly changed direction and ran towards a dark drift to their left. Munashe knew that he was not thinking. There were such moments when one did not have sufficient time to think and could only act from instinct. The instinct to survive. They ran in loping strides for a long time and they continued to hear sporadic fire behind them and then there was a hail of fire from somewhere ahead of them and the night flicked and shone in the powerful searchlights and they returned fire haphazardly and the ground shook with the staccato sound. They changed direction once more, away from the fire, and they ran and ran and ran and there was gunfire everywhere and Munashe saw that the eastern sky was beginning to glow and he knew that daylight was approaching and he began to worry because he knew that if daylight caught them before they crossed the border, they might never be able to make it. Meanwhile, his clothes dripped, drenched with soaking sweat.

Then Tichatonga screamed, clutching his stomach and in the still dim glow of the searchlights, Munashe saw that the man had been disembowelled and instinctively he stopped but the wounded man waved him forward: 'Go on!' His scream was eery, his eyes shone in an abnormal manner, his look spoke of death and Munashe took the magazines from Tichatonga's bandolier before he ran on blindly after Garikayi. All he could remember of Tichatonga was his shirt as it turned crimson with blood and he cried a little inside because one of his two men had met with his fate. And daylight found them deep inside the thick bush of the dry Bopoma River, a short distance away from the border.

Then the helicopters came and they flew in huge circles and their noise made the earth vibrate and Munashe wished they could get to the border. And then they ran into an ambush and there was a barrage of fire from the bank of the dry riverbed and they shot back wildly and Munashe was worried because he knew they would soon run out of ammunition. Then Garikayi screamed somewhere behind a thicket and Munashe knew what had happened to him and he cursed because he no longer cared about anything or anyone and then something strange seized him and he pushed the safety lock of his assault rifle on to full automatic and he stood up and fired from the hip, spraying the other bank with fire and bullets whizzed over and around him but he strode on boldly because he no longer cared and he fed the last fully charged magazine into the chamber of his gun and pushed the safety lock back to semi-automatic and he hit the clumps of bushes on the other side of the river with short bursts of fire and there was dust everywhere so he sprinted down the riverbed not knowing that he had run out of ammunition.

It was only when he came face to face with a Rhodesian soldier, his FN rifle pointing at him, the morning sun dancing on his brown and green camouflage, that he knew that his magazine was empty. And then he was afraid and his AK slipped to the ground.

'Pick it up,' the soldier said calmly, as if he were not interested in the killing and dying surrounding them. Munashe stood motionless, as if he had turned to stone.

'I said pick it up!' the Rhodesian repeated, and Munashe detected the note of urgency in his voice and he hesitantly bent down and picked up the gun.

'Now pass on,' he said. Munashe remained standing. 'I said pass on,' he exclaimed angrily, as if his patience was exhausted. 'You do not have time to waste.'

In a bewildered daze, Munashe moved forward.

'Not that way,' the soldier called after him impatiently. 'We're over there.' He pointed to the right with his gun.

Munashe did as the man had instructed but he felt confused. He kept looking back uncertainly and the Rhodesian kept waving him on angrily, urgently. A short distance ahead, he could see a small hill with a white beacon on top: the border.

By the time he reached the hill, he was struggling to suppress the howl curling, horrible, inside his chest. He did not want to weep for his dead comrades, no. He did not want to weep for anybody. He wanted to weep for himself for his decision to join the horrible, horrible war. Four days later at a FRELIMO base inside Mozambique, it was officially established that out of the thirteen guerrillas from the Chimanda detachment who had attempted to cross the border, only two made it. There might have been three but the third detonated an anti-personnel mine and blew off half his left leg as he crossed the border. The Rhodesians finished him off. It was at the FRELIMO base several kilometres inside Mozambique that the two were disarmed and the base commander informed them that they would be taken to Tete where the rest of their comrades were being held.

'Why are they being kept at Tete? What is happening?' Munashe asked.

'Orders from Lourenço Marques *camarada Zimbabweano*,' the FRELIMO commander said.

'Do you know what it was like at the front without reinforcements? Are you aware how many comrades have died because we were without support?' Munashe continued, angry.

'*Camarada Zimbabweano*, the transitional government in Lourenço Marques has instructed me to disarm *todos Zimbabweanos aqui na Estado do Mocambique* and take them to Tete and this is what I'm doing. I am a soldier, not a civilian administrator.'

'There is no need to remind me.'

And now the other man, the one with the bruised look, raised his gentle eyes from the ground to ask Munashe:

'So you remember?'

'I think I do,' Munashe said. The man smiled. It was a haunting smile and Munashe felt both emotional and confused. Should he thank him for his inexplicable, his generous gesture of a decade ago? Could that act of kindness be sufficiently acknowledged by the words, 'Thank you'? And then the man hugged him like some long-lost-just-found friend and his turmoil increased.

'You don't live around here. Where are you going?' he asked.

And he replied giving his uncle's name and address.

'You don't visit each other very often, do you?'

'Why?'

'He has moved to another village not far from here. I can take you there.' There he was, the same man, again offering to help him.

50

'Won't it take you out of your way?' Munashe said nervously. 'Just give me the directions. I am sure I can find my way.'

'How's life in Harare?' the man asked, ignoring Munashe's discomfort. Then he smiled. That exhausted smile; those liquid eyes; their bruised look! It seemed like yesterday, the desperate Bopoma battle, Tichatonga's bowels, the mysterious Rhodesian rifleman, the horrible war. He did not even know the man's name.

'My name is Godfrey Munetsi,' the man said as if reading Munashe's mind.

'It was an awful time,' he heard himself saying.

'Just like yesterday,' the man said. Munashe grew tense as if they were slowly reliving the awful battle. Why had the man let him through the last line of Rhodesian soldiers especially when he must have seen that he was out of ammunition?

'How is your brother in Harare?' It was a deliberate diversion.

Munashe tensed. 'Do you know him?' Since he returned from the war, Munashe's relationship with his brother had deteriorated. On his last visit, the young man had condemned Munashe as a write-off, a man who could not manage his own life.

'Your uncle is not home,' the man said. Was it another deliberate diversion? Munashe wondered.

'He promised to meet me. He will come.'

'He will not come,' the man said emphatically.

'How do you know?'

'I know,' he said calmly, leading Munashe towards the village where he said his uncle now lived.

Damn my uncle, Munashe cursed. Damn my brother, he cursed again. It was important that he saw his uncle. He wanted to prove to his brother that he was still in control of his life. He wondered why his uncle had agreed to come from Gweru, where he worked as a manager in a shoe manufacturing factory, if he

51

could not make it. How did the ex-Rhodesian soldier know that his uncle was not coming?

'And he might not be able to help you,' the man continued calmly. 'Things are difficult these days. Although your brother should be more sympathetic, don't blame him. Only those who were in the war can understand it.'

'What are you talking about?' Munashe asked, alarmed.

'If it's employment you want, I can help you.'

Munashe was silent. Employment was what he wanted to see his uncle about. He looked at the man closely: what sort of a person was he? Where did he come from?

'I come from Chibwe village near the mission.' Munashe looked at him. Was he dreaming?

'Leave Harare and go to Mutare. Go to Mutare Timbers along the Vumba Road and ask to see Mr Vincent Ncube. Tell him I sent you. He will be able to help you.' And he took Munashe's hand and it was once again the war, the man urging him to move on.

'That's your uncle's home across the stream,' the man said, pointing. 'I am returning but please don't forget what I said.'

'Why are you doing all this for me?' he asked, feeling himself crumble under the weight of memories. When at last he took hold of himself, the man had gone. And his uncle from Gweru did not return home.

He travelled all the way from Harare to Mutare to see Mr Ncube about a week later, all the way in the fetid, overcrowded bus, through open commercial farming areas, through the rich brown country dotted with isolated clumps of *musasa* trees; past countless heads of grazing, rheumy-eyed cattle; past the occasional baboon scampering across the tarred road, looking over its shoulders with frightened eyes, a baby clinging on its underbelly; the sun playing softly on the hills, the trees and the yellow-brown grass; the bus ground on along the straight road narrowing into the horizon. The flat monotonous drumming rhythm, the flat brown country, the hills and the trees began to fill Munashe's mind with curious illusions about what it was like in the forests, the mountains and the rivers during the war. But if at the back of his mind he fought a desperate war, he felt that really there was nothing wrong with him.

And he slowly drifted into sleep and was immediately plunged into a nightmare at Nyadzonia with Kudzai, the day after the massacre. He felt again his horror at the sight of the countless dead and maimed bodies but the corpse that seemed to stand out was that of a young woman with a dead baby on her back: it brought back the memory of the woman standing calmly in her shallow grave gently rocking the baby keening on her back and a sharp pain pierced his heart and the pain clove to the roof of his skull and he heard a single shot and he screamed and the old woman sitting next to him leapt from her seat and all the passengers turned and stared at them in astonishment, and outside the mountains that surrounded Mutare beckoned, and from Christmas Pass they saw the town lying supine in the valley below, as if it was hiding.

He found Mutare Timbers very easily and Mr Ncube the finance manager was indeed there.

'You say you were referred to me by a Godfrey Munetsi from Musami. I don't remember anyone by that name. In fact, I have never been to Musami in my life.'

'But he talked about you.'

'That's strange,' said Mr Ncube, 'but, as it is, one of our accounts clerks resigned without notice yesterday. Do you have any accounting skills?'

God! The Rhodesian soldier from the horrible war!

'Why didn't you complete your economics degree after the

war?' Mr Ncube asked, his voice full of concern. Munashe did not answer. Mr Ncube shrugged and Munashe worried that Mr Ncube did not know anyone called Godfrey Munetsi. Each day as he worked through his schedule in the accounts department, the man's memory haunted him. Was he real or was he a figment of Munashe's own mind? The more he thought about it, the more confused he became.

Several months later in the canteen, he overheard two men talking about Musami.

'Does either of you come from Musami?' he asked anxiously.

'I do,' replied the shorter one.

'My uncle lives near there but unfortunately I am not familiar with the area. I have only been there once.'

'I come from Chibwe,' the short man said.

Munashe felt his heart jump and the short man noticed his heightened interest.

'Why?' he asked.

'I used to know someone from your village.'

'Your uncle?'

'No. Someone else. Godfrey Munetsi.'

'Ho-o, that one,' he said dismissively, 'but he died almost ten years ago.'

'What?' Munashe exclaimed.

'Why . . .? Did you know him well?'

'Did you say he'd died?' Munashe asked.

'Yes. He was my cousin. Most of us advised him to quit the Rhodesian army but he wouldn't listen. Poor fellow. The war was almost over when he came home for the weekend, just a few months before the ceasefire. He had never done so before. Little wonder that our elders say that death lures us on. In any case it was stupid of him. The guerrillas got wind of his presence from the *mujibhas* and they shot him. He was left in the sun in the middle of the village for nearly a week. You could smell his decomposing corpse from a kilometre away.

'When the guerrillas finally gave us permission to bury him, we heaped together what still remained of his body and buried that. Our faces were screwed up in disgust – I mean because of the decomposed body, not the man. It was a long time before I could eat meat again.' He shivered as if he would vomit. 'He should have never come home.'

'Are you certain he died?' Munashe said, hardly above a whisper, sweat forming all over his body.

'*Shamwari*, he was *my* cousin. Is there something wrong with you?'

'No,' Munashe replied uncertainly but nothing felt the same.

'That's how we found ourselves in Mutare, Mother. It was on the instruction of a mysterious man, a ghost. Can you believe it?'

'I can't,' her mother snapped back.

'But as long as the nightmares are confined to the night,' the young woman continued, ignoring her mother's flat denial, 'we can manage. What I dread is that one day he will see what he sees in his sleep when he's awake. Then he will have turned the last corner . . . You will never understand these things, Mother, because you were never involved with them.'

The old woman shrugged her shoulders and said: 'It's all the President's fault. He brought this outrage upon us. Now children act as if they had dropped from the sky and not from the womb of a woman. That man of yours! He will make you turn that last corner with him. And when that happens, don't say I didn't warn you.'

One day on a visit to one of their few friends in Dangamvura, another of Mutare's sprawling townships, Munashe and his wife came upon a man who had prepared the head of an ox, flaying the head and removing the horns. Munashe marvelled at how neatly the man had done the job. Then the man took the handle of an axe to crack open the skull. Blood and broken bone scattered in all directions. And then, oblivious to all else, Munashe jumped over the gate, grabbed the unsuspecting man from behind, and wrenched the makeshift club from his hands.

'Why don't you use a gun?' he shouted. 'It's quicker and less painful.' The man looked at him blankly. Munashe's wife began to pull her husband away, apologizing to the bewildered man. But by then a small crowd had gathered.

And then someone in the crowd began to laugh. 'That man's not mad,' he said. 'That's what Mozambican gold does to you!' He laughed with abandon. 'The Mozambicans treat the *mbanje* leaves with the warm thick soil of the Zambezi where it's been watered for years by baboons. The man's not mad, he smokes a powerful brew!'

Leading her dazed husband by the hand, the young woman drew the man away from the abandoned laughter and the curious eyes that followed them. But she could not hold back the tears that filled her eyes; she could not release the sudden sharp pain of despair.

This was the incident that marked the turning point and confirmed the woman's worst fears. Munashe's nightmares spilled into his waking hours as he sat with his wife in their matchbox house in Sakubva, as he sat at his desk in the dispatch department at work, as he sat on the bus on his way home from work, and they came again at night. His life became a sequence of nightmares: horrible confused disjointed memories of the war. At first the memories were general, haphazard, random, but eventually they focussed on the woman with the baby crying on her back as he battered her with a hoe with a broken handle. She became his daytime nightmare.

The finance manager wrestled with Munashe, struggling to pin him against the wall, shouting for others to come and help him, and at last they subdued him. And a short while later, as he watched the company truck carrying the delirious man to his home in Sakubva, the finance manager felt pity especially for the man's wife. He wondered, as he had often wondered before, how she managed to bear such an enormous burden.

'I am making arrangements to take him to his parents in Mhondoro. They should be able to help us,' the young woman had told him just a month before.

'When you are ready, tell me so that I can grant him the necessary leave days. He is a clever hard-working person and the company needs him. I am sorry for you, Mrs Mungate. You have a real problem on your hands. Doesn't he have a brother to assist you?'

Mrs Mungate shrugged her shoulders. That was another story.

As the finance manager walked away from the window back to his desk, he decided to pass through Sakubva to find out if their arrangements to go to Mhondoro had gone ahead as planned. He was worried because the man's condition seemed to be getting worse by the day. Something had to be done to save him.

PART TWO

That evening's fire had died down and what remained in the hearth were the cold ashes. The yellow flame from the wick of the old paraffin lamp perched on a massive clay-pot flickered weakly, making the dark shadows of the people inside the rondavel quiver ghostlike on the earthen walls. The people's disjointed discussions were drained by the long wait and they whispered wearily, their heads bowed. The jaded voice of the old man of the house, *va*Mungate, could be heard above the sluggish murmur, blaming himself for what was happening, saying for the hundredth time that what was happening tonight should have happened when the child returned from the war in spite of what he may have thought or felt about it because ghosts of war could find a roost long after the war had ended. They were waiting for the first cock-crow. This was the time when, it was believed, the most senior ancestral spirits tottered out of the other world, their frail bodies and gnarled hands resting on their walking-sticks, to cast custodial glances at the children they had left behind and perhaps accept an offering of beer from an anxious child. It was therefore the only time to meet and talk, sometimes briefly, with them during such occasional excursions. They waited for the *bira* to begin.

The leader of the group of the mbira players, sitting next to *va*Mungate, yawned and ran his middle finger carelessly over the keys of the mbira fixed firmly inside the calabash boom and the sound of the keys leapt out of the boom and flew around the room and out through the thatched roof. The player on the rattles shook them wildly above his head while humming a popular traditional tune and the drummer rolled the drum. What surprised Munashe was the control the man had over his hands: he moved them deftly, as if they were made of elastic. They all waited impatiently.

*Va*Mungate's wife, Munashe's mother, whispered something into Munashe's wife's ears and they both shrugged. And *va*-Mungate's eldest sister, *vatete* Nyagadzi, through whom the revered spirit of the family spoke, Manhokwe the lioness, inhaled another pinch of snuff, sneezed, once, twice, thrice and emitted a deep-throated grunt, her thin shoulders shaking vigorously, the tremor running like a current through her body. Everyone waited. Munashe saw them all clearly: next to her husband, his sister from Rugare moving rhythmically to a song inside her head; his sister-in-law next to her, still and subdued. He wondered whether Jonathan, his young brother, her husband, would make a last-minute entrance.

Surprisingly, ever since leaving Mutare two days before, he had had no visits from the ghosts of war. But he had felt strangely light-headed as they stood in silence at Musikawehuku, the town's long distance bus terminus, waiting to board the bus early in the morning. The air was cold and damp, the place dark and deserted; bits of strewn paper blew in the light breeze, while the dark houses of Sakubva, a short distance away to the west, formed eerie silhouettes against the heavy western sky. In the early morning, Mutare looked and felt quiet and calm: its character seemed to stand out strongly: cold, lonely. His wife had insisted that they should board the earliest bus to Harare so that they would not miss the late afternoon buses to Mhondoro. It was a tight schedule.

The bus came and they climbed silently on board, and after the conductor had loaded their baggage onto the roof and tied it down, the bus pulled away from the terminus and droned up Christmas Pass. Munashe looked out of the window at the dark night and saw the small town, still asleep, snuggled in the valley below, its myriad constellations of yellow, blue, red and green fluorescent lights flickering like precious stones taken from the country's womb. He saw the yellowing eastern sky set against the dark mountains standing behind the town; and he felt the thick sheet of floating mist through which the bus bore its way as they climbed higher and higher towards the top of the pass. There, at last, day had broken and Munashe observed the hunched farm buildings, their lights glowing, and farm workers walking briskly on their way to the fields; but it was only much later, on the bus from Harare to Mhondoro, that he was able to enjoy the lavish scenery on both sides of the road.

All the way from Harare, down through the Beatrice commercial farming area, the land on both sides of the road was occupied by highly mechanized farms whose homesteads with their satellite dishes showed through the last butterflied bauhinia flowers, flouncing purple bells of a profusion of jacarandas, and the bright red of a few early flamboyants, and swaying blue gums. Across the Mupfure River, a short distance beyond the small farming town of Beatrice, the rolling landscape was punctuated by monstrous combine harvesters stream-rolling across a field and a cheese-making factory on a dairy farm not far away. Here and there, shoulder to shoulder in neat rows, stood the freshly whitewashed matchbox houses of the farm labourers dappled in the shadows of the pink-leaved *musasa* and an occasional flat-topped acacia.

And then about twenty kilometres off the Beatrice Road, along the road leading to Mamina Dam, the strip-tar came to an abrupt end and neglect and deterioration set in. It showed in the road's state of disrepair: the corrugated ridges zigzagging across the road, the deep mounds of dangerous sand at the edges and the narrow, hanging, derelict bridges. Munashe could tell, even with his eyes closed, that they had left the commercial farming area. But what he might not have realized, had he not known the area, was that farms earmarked for resettlement lay idle in the surrounding land.

Soon, as he sat in the dust-laden bus, he felt the rapid transition of the landscape as they bumped past those farms that had already been resettled. And when the old bus finally crossed the narrow bridge slung low across a heavily silted river, his eyes were stung by the sight of familiar grass-thatched huts, overgrazed pastures, and depleted forests whose remains lay in the small heaps of firewood along the road. Then he knew – and he felt the familiar jolt of painful recognition and acceptance – that they had entered the Jomupani settlement area: land occupied by his people. And then, the Kadhani communal lands.

As they crossed the dry river, Munashe felt an unexpected surge of his old anger as he looked at the tired communal land, and wondered how anybody – how his people – could be expected to eke a living out of such denuded and barren earth. And then through the window he saw a dust-devil spiralling from the naked land, lifting tufts of thatching grass from the huddled huts and tossing it into the arid sky before being swallowed up by distance. The huts followed winding paths that seemed to lead nowhere save to the remnants of another relentless drought. A dry and overcrowded land. Scattered acacia bushes were the only living things breaking the monotony. The blue Ngezi hills to the east stood like bewildered sentinels watching over the ravages of a land without rain. His sense of pain and loneliness was as familiar as his feelings about the war.

As they crossed the Ngezi River, Munashe prayed silently that the sluggish river, hampered as it was by weed and sand, would not decide to stop flowing and dry up, tired. A woman with a baby on her back stood on the bank talking to another woman across the baleful green water. To Munashe, they appeared to be talking to the river, pleading with it to continue flowing. And in the sky above them, the sun burned fiercely. Nothing spoke of promise. The tired villages stretched into the distance, limp and motionless, as if they too had given up living a long time ago. Munashe strained his eyes to have a closer look at a group of people talking to each other by the road side to see if there was anyone among them whom he knew: he was home.

As he grew up, his idea of home was that of a place that was unstable. It had begun when they were living in the area that later became the Lancashire Estates. They returned from the pastures one afternoon to find baton-wielding policemen and green government lorries surrounding the village, waiting to ferry them to another area because the authorities wanted to carve out cattle ranches in the area. Suddenly there was no longer any rabbit and mouse-trapping in the vast open plains as they grazed cattle in the rolling grasslands punctuated by clumps of flat-topped *accacia* trees. And grandmother's folk stories by the crackling fireside in the evenings.

'*Zvakati zvikati*,' she began.

'*Dzepfunde*,' the little children chorused back.

'There was once a poor old widow with only one child, a son. Because she had scoffed at all attempts to give her a second husband, the other villagers thought she was strange and mysterious. They did not trust her. So the chief banished her to the extreme end of the clan where it was presumed she and her son would be the first targets of the enemy. There she lived with her son and there the young man taught himself how to fight using a spear and a club. Then, one day, the enemy came and the old woman began to sing:

'"*Nhai* Mukuku *mwanangu, nhai* Mukuku" for the name of the young man was Mukuku.

'And the young man, being now possessed of some strange spirit, answered back: "*Nhemera*."

63

' "*Pfumo rasvika mwanangu, pfumo rasvika.*"

' "*Amai ndinesimba ndini gonoribaya bu-u-u*" the young man responded.

'And each time the young man said *bu-u-u*, he would lance the enemy with his spear and they fell down in their hundreds until the few that remained turned their backs and fled to where they had come from but Mukuku pursued them and lanced them with his spear until they all perished.

'When he heard about this, the chief was astounded by the young man's bravery and he immediately dispatched a powerful delegation to bring the young man and his mother before his court. After listening with disbelief to the young man's tale, the chief appointed him his closest adviser in direct line of succession and his mother the consultant of the chief's first wife, *vahosi*.

'So you see children, sometimes you have to fight to reclaim your dignity.'

What hurt Munashe most about their eviction was his puppy, Machena. Because the translocation was abrupt and hurried, the small animal was left behind. For over a month at their new home near Tsikiti mountain, he grieved for the loss of his puppy Machena, and refused to talk to anybody. But a year had hardly passed when again they were moved to make way for the Wiltshire Estates.

'Not again!' his mother moaned.

'Why don't we refuse?' Munashe asked his father. The man looked into the horizon, shrugged his shoulders and walked away. And once again, they were translocated, this time to Mhondoro on the banks of the Ngezi River, but Munashe lived with the permanent uncertainty and fear that one day baton-wielding policemen might again descend upon the village and drive them away to some other place to make way for more European farms; home, a place where one stayed with one's bags packed.

Then at last, there was a flap of wings outside, the cock crowed, everyone inside the hut sat up, the lead mbira player struck the keys of his instrument and the other members of the band followed him because it was their way of searching for a way to begin, untangling the cobweb of the present, and then the song swirled out, *Zeeretsi*, the wandering spirit, and *vatete* Nyagadzi struck the lead, setting the sorrowful mood.

She was Munashe's tormented soul making a desperate plea from the wilderness, first to his wife and then to everyone around, as to how they could watch him wander helplessly from hill to hill, village to village, river to river, following forest paths that did not lead anywhere and yet do nothing about it. How much longer would they stand idle whilst he agonized? The music rallied. The drum carved a fierce refrain and *va*Nyagadzi saw the fierce storm approaching from the mountains. Munashe's wife let out a piercing ululation and *va*Nyagadzi stood up and began to stamp her thin legs on the earthen floor. Then she advanced menacingly like a lioness towards the storm. Munashe's sister also let forth a night-shattering ululation. The journey had begun.

To Munashe, the end of the war, signalled by the signing of the Lancaster House peace agreement, was an inexplicable non-event. He watched the other guerrillas and villagers intoxicated by the news and shrugged his shoulders. Several years later, he would attempt to explain not only to his wife but also to himself why he had felt the way he felt:

'To those of us who have been involved in the fighting for over seven years, the war was like a monster whose head and tail none of us could envisage: something with neither a beginning nor an ending. It was almost impossible to imagine that we could outlive the war. At Dzapasi, I met someone whom I had fought alongside in Mount Darwin. The man, shaking his head in disbelief, kept repeating that there was no way the war could have ended because he was still alive. I too felt that way.'

Because the war ended when he was operating in Buhera in the south east of the country, the nearest assembly point was Foxtrot; the local people called it Dzapasi. Even there, he waited to feel the thrill that he knew ought to come with the knowledge that the war had ended; he waited for the prospect of independence to tickle his senses: but the news remained illusively outside and beyond him. But soon his indifference was overshadowed by the disturbing scenes of parents who thronged the assembly point looking for their children who had joined the war years previously. They arrived throughout the day: in the morning, afternoon and evening; Munashe could tell that they were coming from all over the country by the range of their dialects. They came by bus, by car and on foot. And it was not long before Munashe noticed that beneath their outward happiness, and the translucent light in their eyes, behind their inebriated singing as the buses and lorries rolled into the assembly point, beneath their wild embraces as fighters met their people, they all looked the same: anxious, uncertain, afraid. It showed in the way their eyes searched silently, repeatedly, through the guerrilla ranks. It showed in their frayed voices as they talked to the guerrillas about what a burden the war was now that it was over and they would soon be free. They did not ask directly about the whereabouts of their own sons and daughters whom they could not see at the assembly point with the other guerrillas. Instead they asked whether the guerrillas at Dzapasi were the only ones left from the long liberation war. Even as they asked the question, fighting to suppress the pain in their voices, one could begin to detect the panic in their eyes. To them, it was clear that victory and independence would be empty and meaningless if their own sons and daughters did not return home: that was the paradox of the war. They left the assembly point silently, feet dragging, throbbing heads held low, clutching in their limp hands paper bags that contained the provisions that they had brought for the children they had hoped to find. Others, fighting back tears, gave the provisions away to other, more fortunate people's children who had survived. What had the fortunate people done that they hadn't done?

'Your son could be at Dendera in Mudzi or at any other assembly point. There are many assembly points,' Munashe told the old woman but he could see that she did not believe him.

'There is no need to be afraid, my son,' the old woman said. 'We have become accustomed to death. Tell me, is he still alive?'

'I don't even know him, Mother. We were so many out there. Thousands of others are still in the camps in Mozambique. He is alive.'

'Then whose children were they that we saw dying in battle and those we were told were massacred at Nyadzonia and Chimoio?'

Munashe shook his head. He felt helpless before her pain.

'Take these sweet potatoes and roasted groundnuts and eat them. You are the son that I shall never see.' And she walked away as the others had done before her.

The few parents who met their children embraced and hung on to them for a long time almost wordlessly. Then they held each other at arm's length and looked at each other for a long time and cried like little children, turning the dreamy reunion into a tragedy of a kind.

It was that incomprehensible sense of tragedy brought about by both finding and not finding children that prompted Munashe to take the decision that he would not go home, neither would he tell any of his family that he had returned from the war. He would not go home. What with all the death and killing and blood on his hands, could he return home to begin his life all over again, pretending that nothing had happened? No, he would not go home. He could not go home. He would return to the place that represented the most violent part of his life during the war and attempt to reconcile himself quietly, on his own, with the ghosts of the war. He would return to Chimanda. And then an inexplicable sense of urgency gripped him and he saw Chimanda beckoning him and he shouted: I am coming – and somewhere in his mind, he began to believe that there was a task that he had left uncompleted in Chimanda and as he absent-mindedly continued to assure the stream of mothers and fathers trekking into the assembly point about the possible survival of their sons and daughters, his words felt increasingly hollow and he wondered whether anyone believed them and then his sense of futility grew and expanded; and through all this what kept his mind intact was the thought that he would soon return to Chimanda. But what he could not reconcile was the naked juxtaposition of celebration and grief throughout the assembly point. Was either one of the two emotions false? If so, which one? he wondered. Was he sane? Yet needling through his overwhelming sense of futility was his obsession to return to Chimanda.

Thus, as he watched the other guerrillas write urgent letters home, telling family members about their whereabouts, he wondered whether his sister, the last person that he had talked to on that fateful night that he departed for the war nearly ten years before, was still living in the Railway's black township of Rugare.

From a distance, the township looked old and derelict. Its matchbox houses huddled together in sad squat rows like people at a funeral. The rays of the setting sun slanted through black smoke that rose from the chimneys and trailed briefly in the gathering dusk before it mixed with another blanket of thick smoke belching from the factories of the city's west end industrial sites. Not far to the east, the trains shrilled and thundered in the shunting yards. Munashe paused and looked at the township's sad lifeless houses and their amber-coloured bricks, the peeling walls, showing through the shabby curtains the gloom of yellow candlelight, the countless broken-down vehicles sitting on bricks and not wheels in front of some of the houses, the children playing in the poorly-lit streets. He wondered how some people could live with such deprivation and still pretend that things were normal. He could not and that was why he was going to the war to fight to change it. But how would he break the news to his sister? He hesitated before knocking on the bleached door.

'*Ndiri kuuya*,' a female voice answered from inside. The house was old and surrounded by tumbling weeds that swayed in the breeze.

'Munashe!' she exclaimed, opening the door and embracing him. '*Pindayi zvenyu*.' She closed the door behind them and led him to the lounge. Munashe looked around the room; it revealed the family's poverty: a worn-out lounge suite, a cracked pine coffee table, a display cabinet with a broken mirror that reflected false rows of the few water-glasses and plates inside, an old supersonic radiogram, and a black and white television set that had been sent for repairs on several occasions: things he had seen on all his previous visits. The only recent addition was a cheap multi-coloured carpet that covered half of the floor of the lounge, a gift that the husband had got from a retired white Railways friend. What sort of fate determined that his people should be condemned to live like this? No! Something had to be done to change all this.

'How are your studies at college?' she asked.

Munashe did not answer, only fidgeted on the sofa, feeling irritation rising inside him as he realized that he no longer

69

remembered his carefully rehearsed lines. His sister looked at him suspiciously. 'Is anything the matter?'

Suddenly, he felt overwhelmingly tired, a fuzziness in the head and an urge to escape. He felt cornered.

'How is my *mukuwasha*?' he heard himself asking off-tangent.

His sister continued looking at him suspiciously and then after a pause answered: 'He is still with the Railways. Where else would he go?' she added and then again, 'Is everything all right?'

Then he threw away his carefully rehearsed plan and blurted: '*Tete*, I am going away tonight and we might not see each other again for a long time.'

The woman dropped her knitting and stared at him. 'What are you talking about?' she asked calmly, but he could feel the tension in her voice.

Impulsively he jumped up and moved along the narrow passage towards the toilet at the end of the house. He bolted the door behind him. He felt sweat trickling down his back. His sister followed him to the door and banged on it, asking him what he had meant. He held his breath, confused. She kept banging on the door, demanding to be answered. He took a deep breath, unbolted the door and slid out. She grabbed him.

'Please! Let us go back to the lounge and talk sitting down,' he said.

She listened to him calmly and then asked: 'But why?' looking directly at him. 'Why do you want to bring so much pain and suffering to us by abandoning your degree and joining something as risky as the liberation war? Why should you sacrifice your life for something so impersonal, something that does not belong to anybody?

'And when you are eventually killed, who will mourn your loss? Who will cry for you? Who will bury you? Why should you

70

carry the burden of the nation on your head? Just tell me why, my brother.'

'That is precisely our problem. We're always waiting for someone else to do the work for us,' Munashe said, standing up. He picked up his travelling bag.

'Where are you going?' his sister asked.

'I am going to the station to board the eight o'clock train to Bulawayo. We should be in Botswana by this time tomorrow. I am sorry *tete*, there is nothing else I can do. Tell everyone that.'

She held him by the arm as if to stop him and there was a brief tussle but she soon let go and began crying. He walked away, determined not to look back, and disappeared around a corner.

It was her husband who later followed him to the railway station. Munashe saw him coming and moved towards him. 'So you have decided to go?' He paused as if he expected to be answered. 'I just want to let you know that life is meant to be lived and not to be mindlessly thrown away.' Munashe was surprised. The man continued: 'I have not followed you to try to stop you. I followed you to try to make you understand what you are throwing away – a degree, a career, a life. Have you thought at all about what suffering you will cause your family?'

Then the station's public address system announced the departure of the Bulawayo train and Munashe jumped on board as it started to pull away. He looked out through the window and saw the man still standing on the platform and he waved at him but the man did not return his salutation. And as the train gathered speed, he saw the man run briefly after it, stop, shake his head and throw his arms into the air. The last thing he saw was his back as the man walked away. He looked through the window at his blurred image, watching it grow smaller and smaller until it disappeared.

The train rattled out of Salisbury, past the Lochinvar shunting yards, past Rugare township and Munashe thought he saw the forlorn image of his sister standing by the door of her dilapidated house, past the silos of the Grain Marketing Board rising high into the dark night like primordial monsters, past Mufakose township to the right and then into the night, towards Norton.

Then the night was lit by a blinding flash of lightning as *va*Nyagadzi crashed into the storm and the fierce winds swept her from the ground and tossed her into the air and she let out the roar of a lioness, holding out her hand for someone to give her the spear because the duel between nature and nature had begun and Munashe's father saw it and stood up clapping his palms to the fierce rhythm of the music and he began to dance with his eyes tightly shut as if he too was in a trance and the lead mbira player rushed forward and was soon caught up with the drummer and he asked him whether he did not see that the fight had started and the drummer nodded his head to agree and he rolled his hand over the drum once, twice, thrice and the lead mbira player hit his riff keys and Munashe's mother let out a piercing ululation and the lioness sprang into the air roaring and there was absolutely nothing to understand because they were now playing the war song, *Tondobayana*, that warned the other party to the duel, the storm, not to spite other men by calling itself man of men because what each man was worth could only be decided at the end of a gruelling battle. The lioness growled, its canines flashed in the gloom. The storm reared. Outside, the eastern sky began to yellow and the cocks in the neighbourhood crowed alternately: the ancient spirits were on the prowl. Inside, the lioness continued to roar. The music throbbed. And above the music, the hesitant voice of Munashe's father could be heard chanting the praises of Shumba, the lioness, the totem of his people:

> *'Varidzi vesango*
> *Vane meso magwenya*
> *Chishamiso chezvishamiso.'*

Munashe's mother let out a long, unbroken ululation and Munashe began to feel a numbness in the head but he pushed it away for he knew that that was how the ghosts stalked and later pounced and he tried to fix his mind on how beautiful the voice of his mother sounded and likened it to the smooth and sweet and thin but highly intoxicating *mhunga* beer that they drank recklessly in Chimanda at the height of détente.

And it was the potent *mhunga* beer that he thought about for the greater part of his lonely and sorrowful journey from Dzapsai, through Salisbury, back into his past, in a desperate bid to reconcile himself with the blood and the haunting ghosts from the war. The city was a riot of colours and scents and he realized with sadness just how subdued the colours and scents of the African veld were. Tumbling waves of people hurried in all directions as if in response to some powerful invisible force inside them. And Munashe did not detect any celebration at all on their furrowed faces. They seemed preoccupied with other concerns and worries and he wondered what these were. He was happy no one knew who he was. He was ashamed to be associated with the brutal killings, the thoughtless dying in the country in the sun and the festering wounds left by the war. Or was it something that was happening to his mind?

'You are mad!' his young brother had charged one evening during a heated argument at his house in Highfield several years later.

Munashe froze. 'What did you say?' he asked calmly.

'You heard me,' the younger man said mercilessly.

Munashe looked at his moist palms for a long time and then

73

licked the dry roof of his mouth. He stood up silently, picked up his well-kept knapsack and broad-brimmed hat festooned with a lion skin that he had brought from the war, and left. The wife of his young brother saw it from the bedroom window and shook her head.

'What you need is medical help!' the young man shouted cruelly after the hunched, receding figure. Munashe continued walking away, absent-mindedly caressing the edges of his broad-brimmed hat, and soon disappeared into the night. The wife of his young brother moved away from the window and slumped on the bed.

And when he finally arrived in Chimanda late that afternoon, the familiar sight of those hills and kopjes and boulders, the forest and streams, even the trees sent a crazy thrill coursing down his spine and puddles of tears formed in his eyes: it was as if the war had not ended at all. And then he realized with bewilderment that he had not thought of any particular home where he would stay on his emotional return. And then he met her and they remembered each other and embraced.

'Comrade!' she said, her voice quivering with emotion.

'Chenai!' he whispered back. 'How you have grown!'

She cried when he told her that he was the only surviving member of the original Chimanda detachment, and then proceeded to tell him that the war had come to her only brother and sister and they had perished one night when the Rhodesians attacked the village because the soldiers suspected that the comrades were there. She had survived but – she touched the closed eyelid with her hand – 'something gouged my left eye out as blindly in the dark we ran away.'

And then she went on to tell him that her father had died a few months later when his ox-drawn cart detonated a landmine on his way to the grinding mill at Rushinga. And she led him down a forest path to her home to meet her mother and as he walked behind her, he realized that she had aged beyond her years and then suddenly she looked at him and said, 'If the war had continued for another year, no one would have survived. People here do not believe it has ended.'

Outside her home, she pointed at the anthill. 'That is where they all are, my father, brother and sister. That is where we buried them.' And then, 'Tell me, were you also at the assembly point at Marymount Mission?'

'No, I am from Dzapasi in Buhera. That was where I was operating when the war ended.'

'Buhera!' she exclaimed. 'That is very far away. Is your home near here then?'

'No. I come from Mhondoro.'

'Mhondoro! That is also a long way away. I have never been to Mhondoro but one of my aunts was married there.' She paused and looked directly into his eyes: 'Why then have you come here?'

'I don't know,' he said, avoiding her eye.

She looked at the slanted rays of the setting sun and then asked, 'Have you been home to Mhondoro yet?'

'Yes,' he lied. He did not know why.

'Then why have you come here?' she asked once more.

'I don't know,' he said.

'Perhaps you have come to see us,' she said in a hushed voice, taking his coarse hand in hers and squeezing it gently. 'Since father died, my uncle has been telling me to leave the war zone and go and stay with him and his family in Bindura. I have always refused, I don't know why. Perhaps I have been waiting for you.' She paused as if she was unsure of what to say next. And then: 'Mother and the whole village will be happy to see you. Let's go.' But Munashe held on to her hand, not completely understanding what was happening, and then almost without knowing it, he pulled her to him and held her tightly and they stayed like that for a long time and then she said: 'You have come back to me, my long-lost gift, one given to me by the war. The war was strange. It took away and it gave at the same time. What else does that?'

And Chenai's mother brewed the strongest *mhunga* beer the village had ever known and people came from all the surrounding villages to drink it, but they could not finish it because it was so powerful that one ladle was sufficient to knock a man down. And they sang war songs and Munashe began to dance as if he was possessed and then he asked for a walking stick and held it as if it was an AK rifle and he pointed it at imaginary enemies and began to shoot from the hip and then he jumped into the air to the fierce rhythm of the music and his wife stood up and joined him and the wife of his young brother let out a series of piercing ululations and the lioness roared, wrestling with the storm, rolling on the floor, and the music throbbed and pulsated. And then the lioness pinned the storm to the ground and the sky flashed and tore apart and there was thunder and Munashe thought it was enemy artillery at Mount Selinda bombarding their positions across the border at Espungabeira and he rushed towards the door to escape but his wife blocked him and he fell down and shook violently whilst his father and mother pinned him down.

'Hold him down!' the lioness shouted breathlessly. 'I have trapped the storm with my bare hands.'

And there was absolute pandemonium because even the drummer could not keep the drum under control, and he lurched as he desperately tried to stop it from running away with the song. Then the song crashed into a ravine that the drum had unsuccessfully tried to avoid, and died. And then there was silence in the hut as Munashe lay prostrate on the threshold and the old man of the house, Munashe's father, began to clap his hands reverently greeting the lioness Manhokwe because she had calmed down and could now be talked to.

'We greet you, great lioness, and thank you for the visit . . .'

'There is no time!' she interrupted *va*Mungate. There was urgency in her voice. 'I see someone dying in a cave,' the lioness said. They all looked at each other.

'It was during the war. A colleague died in the cave. He talks about it,' Munashe's wife said.

'I see people without knees. I see an aeroplane. I hear the sound of thunder. I see death.'

'It was the war, Shumba,' Munashe's father intervened, clapping his hands reverently.

The lioness convulsed and roared. 'Yes, it was the war. I see a woman,' she said.

'There were many women, Shumba,' Munashe's father came again.

'She is not just another woman,' the lioness said.

'With a baby on her back?' Munashe's wife came in quickly from the wings.

'No,' the lioness said emphatically. 'I am not talking about the woman with the baby on her back. There is another woman that I see.'

'Then it must be Chenai from Chimanda, and after the war.'

'I am talking about a woman during the war. I smell her blood here.'

Munashe's wife hesitated. 'She was my sister.' And everyone turned and looked at her, surprised.

And then somehow, the lead mbira player hit the high keys of his instrument and without knowing it, he blazed the trail of the celebration song *Taireva* and everyone got thoroughly worked up, especially Manhokwe the lioness, because she saw that she

77

had unlocked the first door, and everyone stood up and stomped the earthen floor but as *va*Mungate would remark with tears in his eyes a few months later: 'No one then thought the journey, that had started so positively, would end in tragedy.'

There was a river that ran close to the guerrilla holding camp of Tembwe about sixty kilometres north of the Mozambican town of Tete in the direction of Malawi; that was where Munashe met her. They went to the river in the afternoon to try and wash away the pain caused by the stagnation, the futility, and the stifling sense of nowhereness. The war had ground to a halt and there were no signs, even in the distant horizon, that it would resume; it was nowhere in sight. The name Tembwe itself did not mean anything to anybody: it was nothing in the middle of nowhere.

Munashe listened to one of the camp commanders, the agitated security officer who had ordered him to kill the woman with the baby on her back, rave about Kaunda selling out the struggle because he had imprisoned the party's military leadership but he did not pay any attention to him. The man went on in his usual fermented tone to castigate alleged enemy agents in their midst who, together with Kaunda, were responsible for the situation. He ended by warning them that they would be dealt with ruthlessly in the same manner that their leaders, Badza and Nhari, were dealt with. Munashe walked away towards the river. Ever since, more than a month previously, FRELIMO had walked him and his colleague away from the small base across the border first to Tete and then to Tembwe to rejoin the others, he had not understood anything, only the idleness, the waste, the diminishing food supplies (in Chimanda it was the ammunition), and the hunger, but what he found most difficult was the fact that nothing was happening and nobody seemed to have an explanation about why things were as they were.

A huge fire burned perpetually in the kitchen that served the camp but because there was sometimes nothing to cook, people kept looking emptily at the fire as if that would chase their hunger away, but the hunger remained. When the inadequate food supplies eventually trickled in aboard green FRELIMO army vehicles, it was either mealie-meal or soya beans and for days they would eat nothing else until their breath stank as if something inside them was decaying. Munashe was reminded of the stink as Gondo died in the cave at the front and he wondered when the hopelessness of it all would end but all he heard was the shrill voice of a camp commander and the agitated tones of the security chief who had ordered him to kill the woman with the baby on her back because she was the wife of one of Badza's friends, and talk about the need to rid the party of internal enemies; and he was overwhelmed with dejection as he would walk down to the river, past the empty fire and the empty food drums. There he sat on a rock in the sun, his legs dangling in the water, and watched a group of recruits sitting through a tedious political lesson under a *muonde* tree not far away. The uninspired commissar was highlighting the collective bitterness that led the black man to take up arms and fight the white man: he who came in 1890 and pushed the black man into the dry and arid parts of the country blah, blah, blah, and Munashe thought what an over-beaten path! Shit. He stood up and walked further down the river towards a group of women prisoners, under guard, washing their clothes and searching for lice in their wild, unkempt hair; she was among them and their eyes met.

In that brief moment, she seemed so innocent, so disarming that he wondered what wrong she had done to be where she was. Then he thought of the woman with the baby on her back and his insides somersaulted. Not again! There was something fundamentally wrong with the way the war was being conducted. He stole another glance at her. There was a look in her eyes that contradicted her haggard appearance: the worn-out dress, the unkempt hair, the sallow, wind-swept face, the dry, cracked lips, the dimple on her cheek; and her eyes were deep and mysterious. And even as Munashe walked away, they remained with him and he could not understand why she was where she was. He thought about her all day long until her haggard image merged with that of the woman with the baby on her back and Munashe grew anxious. He began having nightmares of a repetition of what he had done to the woman with the baby on her back, only now he was doing it to the woman being held at the camp security. He could not sleep.

It was several days later that something strange happened to him; the woman reemerged in his mind as tormentingly beautiful. The painful way she had raised her eyes to meet his, the proud, sorrowful way she had thrown back her head to withdraw her eyes from him, the way she had drawn her hand out of the water, every small movement of her body held a suppressed grace and elegance that was out of place within the camp and its prison and its problems. What shook Munashe was how much he thought about her and the near-passion that he began to feel for her. He had never felt this way towards a woman before.

So he went down to the river every afternoon in the hope that he would see her when the prisoners were assembled for their daily wash but she was never among them. And then he began to blame himself for his cowardice; he should go to security and ask for her and perhaps help her out; no, he could not do that, had he already forgotten his experience at the training camp in Zambia? He did not know what to do. Meanwhile, as he threw out first one idea and then another, he remembered her eyes, two floating stars in the sky of her wind-swept face, and he tidied a small corner in his mind where he could keep the image safely and securely because it was the only thing about her that he owned. And the war, the woman with the baby on her back, and the ugly situation in Chimanda seemed to recede. Yet the strange thing was that he did not know the woman's name and was afraid to ask anybody what it was.

And then something happened: the woman was released but taken away immediately, along with several commanders who were being transferred to Nyadzonia and Chibavava refugee camps in central Mozambique. As she got in the Land Rover ahead of the security officer who had ordered Munashe to kill the woman with the baby on her back, their eyes met again and he saw that she wanted to tell him something and as the truck drove out of the camp, Munashe's heart sank. It was as if she was taking away a part of himself. And then suddenly, unexpectedly, no matter how he tried, he could not remember what she looked like, even the memory of her eyes had vanished like stars on a bleak night, and in her place the image returned of the woman with the baby on her back, and he wished the war would resume so that he could return to the front, and perhaps to his death. But the war never started and the hopelessness and idleness and waste persisted and because the guerrillas had nothing to do, they ruthlessly turned on each other and meted out severe punishments for the slightest misdemeanour – the favourite of which was called *jato du povo*, a form of punishment borrowed from FRELIMO in which the victim had his arms tied above the elbows behind his back with a piece of insulated copper wire forcing the chest out abnormally so the culprit looked like a chicken being held up by the wings, and he was reminded of the first victim he had seen in the camp outside Lusaka.

The reason why it was called *jato du povo* (Portuguese for the people's jet fighter) was because when it was administered, the victim looked like a fighter plane: the arms and hands formed the wings, the head the nose and the legs the tail. The punishment and the way in which it was administered was harrowing. Munashe felt that such heartless cruelty could only be found in war. *Aizosunungurwa aridza pembe yenhunzi* – shitting in one's pants. Munashe looked at the latest victim, a young man writhing in the hot sun, and saw the bulge that had formed between his shoulders and the wire sunk into the swollen flesh and he walked away from the parade and went down to the river. He wished the war would resume but the stagnation dragged on with the nationalist leaders locked in fruitless political talks in Lusaka whilst the volunteers wasted away in holding camps in Mozambique. And every day he tried to conjure up the memory of the woman comrade down by the river but all he saw were the haunted eyes of the woman with the baby on her back and he fled and took refuge at the river in the place where the prisoner with the kinky hair had knelt as she washed her wind-swept face.

They finally met nearly a year later, the day after the Nyadzonia massacre, at the Pungwe River bridge which had been blown up by the Rhodesian security forces. By then the war had long resumed after the formation of ZIPA and the loose military merger of ZANLA and ZIPRA, and Munashe had almost forgotten everything about her. He was returning from the front for arms replenishment and she was part of the rescue team that had been dispatched from Chimoio soon after the news that Nyadzonia had been attacked. Unable to cross the swollen river most of the survivors of the massacre were gathered at the wrecked bridge. Everyone was too busy attending to them to notice anything else. The story of the massacre was evident in their frightened eyes, their lacerated bodies, their torn clothes. Munashe's eyes met with those of a boy who could not have been more than ten; they were blank and empty. A young woman holding a torn blood-smudged baby shawl, booties and napkin tried to say something. Pointing a trembling hand at the hill behind which lay what once had been a refugee camp and was now only a hint of black smoke against the sky, she began to wail. Munashe looked away and that was when he saw, standing beside him, the mysterious woman from Tembwe whose eyes floated like stars in the sky. He froze. What was she doing there? Where was she coming from? And without knowing why, he slung his AK over his shoulder and walked away. The mysterious woman clutched her gun and walked over to the young woman who continued to cry.

They abandoned the vehicles and proceeded on foot to the camp a few kilometres away. Although Munashe could not see her, he felt her presence above the intense smell of gunpowder as they drew closer to the camp. And then they were overwhelmed by the stink of decomposing bodies and Munashe could think of nothing but death. Corpses were littered everywhere. The tiny abandoned bodies of suckling babies made him think not only of the young woman with the blood-smudged shawl, but also of the woman with the baby on her back.

Whole bodies of little boys and girls, young men and women, old men and old women lay scattered amongst those with severed heads, crushed skulls, shattered faces, missing limbs and shredded stomachs. Flies, swarms of heavy, green flies hovered over the bodies moving from corpse to corpse like helicopters during an attack: the worms had not yet appeared, they could come later.

Then there were the many injured, hundreds of them, groaning in pain. Some had been shot and left for dead and others had their legs and arms crushed by the rumbling steel-belted wheels of armoured vehicles. A small girl with a gaping wound in her small chest sat calmly in a donga. 'Am I going to die, comrade?' she asked. Munashe, unable to reply, turned abruptly away and bumped into the mysterious woman from Tembwe. Wordlessly they held each other and sobbed in silence for something so much more than the little girl with the gaping chest. So they did not see her die. When, finally, they stopped crying, Munashe slung his gun over his shoulder and walked away. The mysterious woman gently picked up the warm body of the little girl and walked towards the mass graves at the edge of the camp. Night found them scouring the surrounding bush for the remaining wounded in order to load them on to the helicopters waiting to ferry them to hospitals in Chimoio and Beira.

That night, none of them ate anything. Instead they slept, dog-weary; sleep blocked out the groans of the injured.

But Munashe heard them and after a time, unable to bear it, he rose and walked down towards the Nyadzonia River and sat on a rock, his legs dangling in the water, his gun beside him. He was surprised that even there he could hear the sounds of the injured and dying. Life and death had become interchangeable. He thought of all the death that he had caused or witnessed in the war which added to his sense of helplessness and of confusion. Then he heard footsteps and turned his head and she stood in the silver light of the moon a few paces behind him and the pale light accentuated her breasts, broad hips and tall slender frame. And then from the bush across the river came the disjointed sound that they both knew of someone struggling to push death away and she sat down beside him and pushed his gun aside and held his hand in hers and he felt her warmth. She whispered something in his ear but he did not hear her words because something inside him melted and their bodies met and the woman cried out as if she too was dying, pleading with him to stop, and he had a brief dream in which both of them had died. And the woman cried and begged him to stop and asked him to stay, pushing him away and holding him back.

A long time later, they lay still on the rocks beside the river, the sound of the dying in the air and he was the first to speak: 'Who are you?'

'The woman with the baby on her back inside the moon is crying,' she whispered and shocked he sat up.

'What are you talking about?' he asked.

'Can't you see her up there?' she pointed at the full moon.

'Why is she crying?'

'Of course you don't know,' she said dismissively. 'Only a woman can understand that mystery.'

'Who are you?' he asked again.

'Nobody.'

'What do you mean?'

'What can you call someone who has had three abortions in one year? My life in the war. What sort of credentials are these? I don't want to be considered anything. I am nobody. I am nothing.'

'What are you talking about?'

'I was raped by the bastard for over a year! I couldn't run away. I had no option but to abort. I *hate* men. I *hate* the war.'

'Why didn't you refuse him?'

'Rape? Refuse? That was why you saw me in prison at Tembwe.'

'Was there no one to help you?'

Her laughter was sarcastic. 'Who?' she asked. 'Perhaps that's why I am telling you. I've never told anyone before. It was pointless. Can you report a superior? Now something strange is happening to me. I no longer menstruate and I am not pregnant. Menopause at twenty!'

'Who is he?'

'He has gone to the front. I hope he's killed.'

'Why are you telling me all this? You don't even know who I am!'

'I don't know why I am telling you all this. I don't know why I joined the war. My name is Kudzai.' And they each began the painful journey back into their past and the air was full of the sound of the dying and the foul smell of death. And above them the moon sailed across the deep dark sky and Munashe saw the woman with the baby on her back and he shivered. It was like a disjointed dream and the sound of anguish in the air kept stabbing at him like the bayonet of an assault rifle and he continued to lie flat on the threshold and Manhokwe the lioness screamed and *Taireva* throbbed out: the celebration continued. Then the music faltered and the song coughed as if it was choking and died away. The lioness continued to roar.

'Speak, owner of the jungles,' Munashe's father implored, crouching on the floor. 'We don't send them on any errand, these ears of your greatness. We have them here with us and they are all yours.' He clapped his hands. 'Speak.'

'What happened to that woman?' She inhaled a pinch of snuff and sneezed.

'He told us that she died at Chimoio,' Munashe's wife said.

'That is correct,' the lioness said. 'She had surrendered but they killed her.'

'That is what he said, your greatness,' she choked with emotion. 'She left nothing, not even a letter. We thought she had gone to Britain since she worked for Air Rhodesia. We could not believe it when he brought us the news that she had been killed in Mozambique.'

The lioness leapt into the air and bared her canines and they flashed in the dull light and she shook her head and the lead mbira player's nimble fingers carved *Njodzi*, and Manhokwe grabbed her spear and leapt into the lead. She cried as she crooned the details of how the victim in the song met with death: she was swept away by a swollen river; she was bitten by a venomous mamba; she was devoured by a lion; she was dragged and eaten by a hungry crocodile; she was struck by lightning; all inevitable natural deaths pitting man against nature, there was no way the poor woman could have survived. Manhokwe was nature fighting against nature. She leapt higher into the air.

'This is the first time I am hearing all these strange stories. What's happening?' Munashe's father interrupted.

'Silence!' snarled the lioness. 'Why did it take you so many years to do what you are doing today? Who were you waiting for to teach you to be the man of the family? Are you still a baby with milk on your nose? Is there anything in those trousers?'

'It's him that refused!' he protested, pointing at the prostrate figure of his son. 'His young brother would have vouched for me if he'd been here.'

The last irreparable confrontation between Munashe and his young brother occurred when he, as usual, had visited the young man at his home in Highfield about five years after the end of the war. Because of the nature of their relationship, he had informed the young man's wife that he would drop by. He had told himself many times that he only visited them because of the woman and her children, especially the little boy Taurayi. However on this occasion he had overheard an argument between the young man and his wife.

'You know how I feel about him!' the young man had said.

'But, Jonathan, he is your *only* brother!' the woman argued, pain in her voice.

'Yes, he is my brother but he is mad and he won't admit it.'

'He is *not* mad! He needs help and if you don't want to help him, who will?'

'He is not mad? Then what do you call a person who wanders from place to place wearing the clothes that he wore in the war? What do you call someone who refused to return to finish his degree, although he was more than halfway through the course work? What do you call someone who refuses to work, who will not get married? What do you call someone who yaps on and on about battles in Chimanda, Buhera and Chipinge during that lousy war, a war which ended years ago? Show me a thousand mad people and I will show you just one. *My* brother! How do you think *I* feel?'

'It's the war which has done this to him.'

' "It's the war!" Give me a break. One of these days, I shall tell him never to set his foot in my house again!'

'My god!' his wife exclaimed, as her eye caught Munashe disappearing back into the night.

This time, he arrived in the afternoon and the first person he saw was the little boy, his brother's eldest son, who always boasted that he recognized Munashe's broad-brimmed hat and knapsack long before he arrived. On more than one occasion, Munashe had told the child that he would one day give them to him and the boy always reminded him of his promise.

Taurayi ran up the street and into the warmth of his uncle's outstretched arms and hearty laughter and then he asked the small boy to carry his knapsack. No one else was allowed to do so. This time, he allowed him not only to carry the knapsack but to wear the hat and so they walked side by side back to the house.

'Growing bigger every day, he-e? Very soon the hat won't fit.' The little boy blushed.

'You mean you will give it to me today?' he challenged.

'Not quite yet! Not quite yet, but pretty soon,' his uncle ducked the question. 'I haven't forgotten,' he added reassuringly. 'How is school?' he asked.

'It's fine. Did you have any schools in the war?'

The uncle laughed nervously. 'Yes, there were schools.'

'I once saw pictures of lots of children killed outside their classroom in Mozambique.'

The man felt cornered. 'Yes, that happened . . . How is everyone at home?' he tried to change the subject.

'Were you ever involved in a battle at a school?' the small boy persisted. Taurayi knew that his uncle had one such story that he had heard many times before but he never tired of it.

The uncle threw his arms into the air dejectedly. 'Yes,' he said.

'How did you survive?' the child's eyes widened.

'By pretending to be one of the teachers,' the man said.

'You will tell the story about how you were shot through the shoulder in Chipinge, Uncle, won't you?'

He was trapped. 'But these are stories for men, Taurayi, not boys.' He paused and looked away: 'But, we'll see.'

And the little boy shouted: 'Hooray!' And side by side, they walked on towards the house.

The township stood still, its hands hanging at its sides, watching them. Taurayi's mother came to the gate to meet them. When Taurayi's father arrived later from work, he walked past his elder brother without even looking at him and shut himself in his bedroom. Munashe wondered whether his brother might not have seen him. He swallowed and waited.

After what seemed a long time, the younger man emerged from his room, whistling softly, and without looking at his older brother, exclaimed: 'O-oh, so it's you? I didn't see you when I came in. *Mai* Taurayi told me you were passing by. When did you arrive?'

The older man felt, as he always did, an erosion of certainty and he steeled himself against the sense of inadequacy that threatened to engulf him. His younger brother kept his face averted, as if the older man was of no importance, no value at all. Munashe swallowed, wishing he was elsewhere. When he felt like this, he had taught himself to withdraw into the background and only answer questions that were put to him. When all the routine replies had been given, the young man asked: 'Have you heard about the government food-for-work programme?' It was a cruel question, crudely put, and the young man felt a vindictive satisfaction.

Munashe was puzzled. If he had been in the kitchen, he would have seen his sister-in-law's hand freeze in mid-air as she added a pinch of salt to the evening's bowl of vegetables. 'Not that I know of,' he replied calmly, then silence fell. Much, much later, still whistling softly under his breath and never having looked at his brother once, the younger man left the room.

During supper that evening, *Mai* Taurayi tried to cheer everyone up, paying particular attention to her brother-in-law. The man, who was visibly upset, slowly relaxed and began to enjoy his steak. His younger brother ate silently, hunched over his plate, as if the meal was a severe trial. Taurayi felt the tension and stole furtive glances at his uncle, his father and his mother.

'Travelling all the way here has made me hungry,' said the older man between mouthfuls.

'Where were you coming from?' the younger man asked heartlessly.

Mai Taurayi glanced at her husband. The man laughed recklessly and shoved a huge piece of meat into his mouth. His older brother stopped eating and looked down at his plate.

'What was it like crossing Devure Ranch and going along the Save River into Bikita during the war?' the little boy asked unexpectedly. The young man suddenly stopped eating and looked at his brother. The older man's lips began to tremble. *Mai* Taurayi looked away. 'You promised to tell me, Uncle! What was it like?'

'Go on! Tell him. Isn't that what you've been doing since the war ended?' the young man said mercilessly.

Munashe pushed away the plate in front of him as if it would get in the way of what he wanted to say. 'It's not that I enjoy telling stories,' he said. *Mai* Taurayi averted her eyes to hide her shame and embarrassment. 'Telling the stories is an ordeal. It's as if the war has begun all over again. It was a horrible time. It's the small boy who likes to hear the stories and I do not want to ignore and hurt him. I tell them for his sake.'

Jonathan laughed mirthlessly. 'And I suppose you will tell us that your perpetual wandering is also done for someone's sake?'

'Please *Baba va*Taurayi!' his wife implored.

'Shut up woman!' her husband banged the table with his fist.

'I move from place to place in an attempt to escape from my memories of the war. One day I hope to leave them behind. But ghosts follow me wherever I go. I don't want to think about the war. I want to forget it, but I can't. Terrible memories get in the way of everything I do.' The man put his face in his hands and began to cry. The wife of his young brother looked the other way, her nails digging into her palms. The little boy began to cry too.

'You're mad, that's all. I have told you this before and I am telling you again.' *Mai* Taurayi opened her mouth to speak but said nothing. Munashe's head was buried in his hands.

'*Mukoma*, it's a fact! *I am telling you.*'

'Don't be so cruel *Baba va*Taurayi.'

'It's the truth which is cruel, not me. Perhaps your memories have to do with the nasty things you did and the innocent blood you spilled. The truth is coming out now, we know it.'

Munashe rose slowly from the table, wiped his face with the back of his hand, pushed back his chair, and walked heavily on to the verandah where he sat in the dull light, staring unseeingly in front of him.

'Look at him! Just look at him,' the young man shouted at his wife inside the house. 'He fought in that stupid war for nearly a decade and what has he got out of it? No compensation because he has no physical injuries. They even dismissed and awarded a nil percentage for the bullet that went through his shoulder. No, not even a thank you. He deserved more! We all deserved more than the corruption which is fast becoming a part of our culture.' He paused. 'And whilst he fought, some people were unashamedly making money out of the war. And now, whilst he drifts from location to location, other people are making millions – millions on the back of their pay-outs, their compensation! Is it his job just to walk and talk putting on the same clothes, the same clothes that he brought back from that war? Today I'm going to tell him I don't want to see him here again. This house is no place for mad men. Taurayi! Call your uncle back.' The young man glanced through the window at his older brother on the verandah and was satisfied that he had heard everything that he had said. Then they heard the sudden shattering sound of a glass falling and splintering into shards on the cement floor. *Mai* Taurayi looked as if she had turned to stone. There was absolute silence in the room.

Munashe did not wait to be called back into the house. He slung his knapsack over his shoulder, held his broad-brimmed hat festooned with a lion skin in his hand and walked out of the gate. Behind him, he heard the sound of breaking glass. Then he felt something small brush gently against his hand and he looked down and he saw the little boy walking beside him and the boy asked: 'When will you come back for your promise?' and Munashe felt his heart turn over and he lifted the small boy and held him close to his chest. He could not hold back the tears that fell from his eyes and when he put the little boy down on the ground, he put the broad-brimmed hat on his small head and said: 'I shall bring the knapsack some other time,' and the small boy leapt into the air in jubilation and rushed back home to show the gift to his parents shouting: 'One day I shall become a soldier fighting in the war,' and his mother saw everything by the floodlight at the end of the street and she called out to Munashe: 'Thank you for the hat. I will make sure he keeps it safely.' And she turned and ran back into the house because she could no longer hold back the howl that was choking her throat and Munashe disappeared into the night and the township stood still and watched him, chiding people like his younger brother for forcing him to endure such humilation because he had fought in the war, pst, pst, pst, and then wondering who the heroes were, or if there were any heroes at all, but Munashe could still manage a wry smile as he reflected on the words that the small boy had shouted as he ran excitedly back home, Munashe's hat in his hands: I will become a soldier and fight in another war!

Another war?

Once on a visit to Dzivarasekwa along the road to Bulawayo, he had seen huge armoured personnel carriers rumble west towards Matabeleland: another war that threatened to tear the country apart had broken out, ZANU versus ZAPU, the Shonas versus the Ndebeles: a civil war!

Munashe clearly remembered how the problem had begun: the discovery, at former ZIPRA assembly points, of huge arms caches, allegedly intended to topple the government. He was returning from the uncompleted journey to Chimanda and moving distractedly across the barren plains, the surrounding villages watching him curiously, when news of the discovery had broken out. Unlike much other news, the situation in Matabeleland disturbed him. Was this the first sign of another war? As he watched the convoy roll by and saw the sweating faces of the young troopers at the back of the armoured vehicles holding their rifles loosely, arrogantly, at the ready, he noticed a familiar madness in the pupils of their eyes, their pursed lips, and felt the air explode with the sickening smell of gunpowder. He quickly turned and walked away. And he thought: war is the greatest scourge of mankind.

'The Ndebeles do not know what war is like because they were never involved in the one that freed the country,' screamed a fat woman behind the makeshift counter of her wooden tuckshop. 'They were building battalions in Zambia preparing for this one. Go and show them what it's like, boys!' she said, waving wildly at the passing convoy. The young soldiers did not wave back. They stared stoically ahead. Munashe shook his head.

Another war?

And he thought: some people made thousands during the war when the cities were flooded with people escaping from the country, the killing and the dying. Did this woman hope to make up for what she had missed during that time? Then he was wrong. There were very few people who thought like him that the war had brought so much pain and suffering that they would shun another war. And then he thought: but the relationship between ZANU and ZAPU has always been violent.

He remembered his first visit to the city when he was still a small boy. It was an accidental journey because it had not been intended that he should go; rather it had been his mother and the baby Jonathan who had been supposed to go to Harare to visit his mother's uncle in Highfield. The night before the journey, he could not sleep; he had also wanted to go to the city. He had tossed and turned, his heart aching. And when day finally broke, the thought that his younger brother and his mother would soon be leaving for the city stifled him. And as his mother packed her bags and left to catch the only bus into the city, he had refused to remain at home and had followed at a distance. Because he had been crying for such a long time, he no longer remembered that he was crying, and his mind wandered on to other things: the school, the veld, and then the city, a complete circle – what was it about the city that had beckoned so powerfully? and he had cried emitting occasional hoarse sounds like hiccups.

At the bus stop, his mother had continued to shout at him while he stood a short distance away. She gestured wildly with her hands and admonished him for wanting to go to Harare instead of to school. Then they heard the bus coming and the noise made Munashe hysterical. He threw himself down in the middle of the road and wailed as if someone had died. And his action had enraged his mother who had torn a small branch from a tree with which to beat him when old Albion had arrived and the driver, who looked just as old as the bus, thrust his head through the window and asked:

'Is he your son?'

'And a stubborn one too!'

'Why don't you let him come with you?'

'And what about school?'

'Are you staying there long?'

'Over the weekend.'

'He won't miss much school. I will give him a free ride.'

That historic visit and its stunning sights – the dazzling flashing neon lights, the endless rows of scuttling motor cars (the only other car which he knew besides the old Albion was a blue Bedford half-ton truck that belonged to Mr Mareto, the businessman who owned a small store), dizzying buildings whose tops brushed the fat white clouds hanging on the blue belly of the sky, and the people, he had never seen so many people – was spoiled when supporters of ZAPU savagely beat his uncle in front of his own house, moments after they had arrived. The window panes of the house had been shattered by stones and the man was left lying in a pool of blood outside the broken gate. The horde marched away singing a song that promised revenge on anyone who dared to join the newly formed political party called ZANU because it was formed by crooks who wanted to trick innocent people out of their money.

The police, a white officer and two black constables, arrived in a grey Land Rover whose windows and headlamps were covered with mesh wire and took the groaning man away.

The following day, they hurriedly returned home to Mhondoro, afraid that something sinister might happen to them. And all the way back on the same old Albion, the little boy Munashe heard in his mind again and again the hideous words of the song that the horde sang as they beat up his uncle:

> ChiZANU tabhana
> ChiZANU chemari
> Makatarisa mose muchiona.

We have routed ZANU because it is an evil party only interested in the people's money and the point is we have done it right in the people's faces!

So that the resplendent impression that he had of the city was replaced by the ugly image of his uncle's bloodied body lying in front of the twisted gate and the horde of young people singing a song of hatred. And for a long time he struggled to find something unpleasant enough to compare Harare with, that is until he joined the war.

Had his uncle survived, he would have told him, but the beating had killed him and Munashe's mother journeyed back to the city. Had she asked Munashe to accompany her, he would have refused.

Another war?

There had also been the shoot-outs which had left scores of

guerrillas dead in the Morogoro and Mgagao training camps in Tanzania, after the two parties had been forced to unite. He was already at the front, but, like many others, he had heard the harrowing details several months later from someone who had survived the shoot-outs by a whisker.

Another war?

Then he remembered a dull afternoon at the front with Lizwe around the time of the shoot-outs in Tanzania. It had only taken a casual conversation for him to realize that the hostile situation in the training camps had spilled over to the front.

'You are so different from the others,' the man had said hesitantly as they sat on a small hill overlooking the Tanganda Tea Estates. 'You don't seem to be aware of the secret instruction.'

'What secret instruction?'

'One of our guys intercepted the instruction from your military command. You are supposed to eliminate us once we cross the border to the front.'

'I have not heard anything like this.'

Many years later, his wife asked how he had managed to live from day to day when he was oblivious to so much information, that to others was common knowledge.

'I had died years before Chimanda. What survived through the war was my ghost.'

'You're a loner, that's why,' Lizwe said. 'Your comrades are suspicious because you are friendly to me. But if it weren't for you, I would have been killed a long time ago or, as instructed by our High Command, I would have found my way back to Zambia to rejoin ZAPU. Indeed I want to run to Zambia. I cannot stay here and survive.'

And Munashe remembered how Sly had come and talked to him just before he deserted. What was it that made people talk to

97

him just before they ran away? But all he said was, 'Will you make it to Zambia?'

'It's war. One way or another we'll all die.'

'Is there anything I can do to help you?'

'I don't want help from anybody. I will go tonight.'

And Lizwe ran away that night, in a desperate bid to cross the entire breadth of the country and return to Zambia and other members of ZIPRA. And silently Munashe wished him luck because he had long since lost any faith in the war.

Strangely, Munashe had met Lizwe in Harare several years after the war. The man was confined to a wheelchair from an injury sustained in the Entumbane shoot-out in Bulawayo between ZANU and ZAPU a few months after independence. And Munashe knew that he had watched the personnel carriers carrying a man who'd carried the gun which shot Lizwe as they rolled towards Bulawayo.

'Unfortunately, I don't qualify for compensation,' Lizwe said, laughing carelessly. 'Technically, the injury occurred after the war.'

As they talked, two people from opposing factions who were on the same side of the war; two people reliving the tragedy of their lives that had begun in that war, Harare rumbled on. It seemed that only people like them knew that beneath the surface, the city was callous, ruthless.

'Is there really any purpose to life?' Lizwe asked.

Munashe wished he knew the answer.

'It's the sores developing on my backside that are the nuisance,' he said hardly above a whisper, and then laughed dismissively. 'They have begun to grow septic,' said the young man who pushed the wheelchair. 'His backside is wet with pus.' Lizwe made as if he wanted to stand up but Munashe stopped him. Every day there were people, situations, war victims, economic victims, beggars, whose needs overwhelmed the individual.

'How I would have loved you to tell me how you got to Zambia! But never mind. I don't think it's important any longer.'

Lizwe shrugged his shoulders and then suddenly there was nothing more to talk about. The invisible, the frightful divide between ZAPU and ZANU had interposed itself.

'By the way, he is my cousin,' he pointed to the young man pushing his wheelchair. 'And this is a friend from the war' he said pointing at Munashe and somehow Munashe felt that everything that there was between them had been said and what now remained was to part and he moved away silently.

'Are you still in the army?' Lizwe called after him.

'No, I have never been in it!'

'Then what are you doing?'

'Nothing,' he answered and he laughed at himself. 'Just wandering,' he continued. 'I'm trying to work off the load that I must leave behind, before I can settle down to anything.'

'At least you have somewhere to begin from. Some of us have nowhere to start from even if with legs. We were condemned by history to be on the wrong side.'

Before he turned the next corner, Munashe looked back and saw Lizwe telling the young man to call him back and their eyes met: how could history be so cruel? Munashe hurried away. And Harare issued a deep metallic roar and vaMungate saw the anger in the lioness' eyes and he suddenly became conciliatory: 'I was only saying if he had been forthcoming when he returned from the war, we could have sorted out the problem a long time ago.'

'Don't argue with me!' the lioness snarled. 'Here we finally are with blood on our hands and without any time on our side and you tell me it was the child who was to blame for this mess. Who do you think I am? Boy, without any hair on the crotch! Don't try me!'

99

*Va*Mungate went down on one knee and pleaded with her to forgive him for his errant words and the lioness shook angrily.

'There is another woman that I keep seeing. Who is she?'

'The one with the baby on her back?' Munashe's wife hurried to say something to diffuse the tension.

'I haven't come to that one yet. There is another woman, with an impaired eye.'

'It is Chenai from Chimanda. She came after the war,' *Amai* Mujura, Munashe's sister, said. Manhokwe grunted, nodding her shaven head in agreement.

Munashe's blissful time with Chenai in Chimanda did not last because instead of the scars of the war littered around the area bringing him relief and some measure of reconciliation with that brutal time as he had anticipated, he felt his suspicions crawl back and he began to be afraid that something might leap out of the nearest bush and pounce on him and Chenai saw it and asked him what the problem was.

'I think I need to go on further,' he replied, looking at the range of the blue mountains across the border inside Mozambique.

'I don't understand.'

'I think I was terribly mistaken,' he said as if he was talking to himself. 'There is no way that I can reconcile myself with the ghosts of the war without beginning in Mozambique. Please Chenai, if you love me, accompany me to Mozambique. My peace begins there.'

'What are you talking about?' she asked, startled.

'The war has ended, Chenai. I need to let go of the burden that I'm carrying. I need to start living again. Please help me. If you can't, then no one can and I might as well go to Mozambique on my own.' Chenai saw the strange light in his eyes and became frightened. For the whole night, she talked it over with her mother but they could not agree. Her mother felt they had to ask the comrades at Marymount Mission to come and fetch him but Chenai, because she was afraid that she would lose him, felt she should accompany him to his people in Mhondoro. But when they woke up the following morning, Munashe had gone.

The search for Munashe began with his sister, *Amai* Mujuru, in Rugare a few weeks after the end of the war. It was not out of hope that the man would still be alive; it was out of a sense of obligation, the kind of desperate effort that people put into looking after a patient although everyone knows the illness is terminal. They were driven by a force that none among them understood. They had to do something; after all, everyone else with a relative who had gone to the war was doing the same thing. *Amai* Mujuru called the members of her family to Rugare.

'It's you that he said good-bye to on the day he left,' Jonathan said, trying to lay the responsibility for whatever might transpire on his sister.

'The question of who he said good-bye to is neither here nor there,' his wife, *Amai* Taurayi, interjected. 'Munashe is not a distant relative. He is one of the family and that is what is important.'

'I don't know why he doesn't want to grow up, this one,' Jonathan's mother said angrily. 'How he still bears the bitterness of being excluded because Munashe did not tell him that he was leaving beats me. Does he think going to the war was like going to a wedding?' But *va*Mungate, his father, never said a word during the sometimes acrimonious discussion which followed.

It was finally agreed that *Amai* Mujuru and Jonathan's wife would follow the uncertain trail to Foxtrot and the two women silently left for the assembly point. And it was there that they were told the dubious news that Munashe was still alive but that he had left a confused message that he was going to Chimanda in

Rushinga to collect something that he had forgotten there during the war and they did not know whether to believe the news or not because it did not seem to make sense and besides they had a suspicion that this was what everyone else was also being told but they nevertheless could not help but follow the trail to Chimanda. So, back in the city a few days later, the two women left for Chimanda, a place that neither of them had been to, to look for a possible war survivor called Munashe. What drove them on was the knowledge that they were not the only ones searching. They had simply become part of a collective madness to search and go on searching, even when the search had become not a means to an end but an end in itself. But unlike the other hopefuls, the two women did not carry provisions for the possible survivor.

'You also aren't sure, are you?' asked *Amai* Mujuru, breaking the silence between them as the old bus plunged east from Mount Darwin, towards Rushinga.

'I am frightened,' her sister-in-law replied.

'Where are we going?'

'I don't know,' Jonathan's wife said.

The futility of their journey came into sharp focus at Rushinga when they disembarked, when they could only stare at each other foolishly because they had nowhere to go because although there were people around, they did not have any specific directions to ask them. Then they saw a man come running towards the bus in the gathering dusk, asking with a wild gesture of his hands whether it was the bus that was proceeding to Nyakatondo on the border with Mozambique at the nose of the great Mavhura-donha mountains and *Amai* Mujuru thought there was something alarmingly familiar about the anxious voice. Then the world froze as they all stood and stared at each other and the first thing that *Amai* Mujuru noticed after all the years of silent uncertainty and painful absence was the frightening abstraction in his eyes, which were empty, unfocussed and unsettling, as if he was thinking about things that were not there, and wherever they were, he did not understand them either.

'Do you see what I see?' *Amai* Mujuru asked late at night back at *Amai* Chenai's home where Munashe had reluctantly taken them to put up for the night.

'Yes,' her sister-in-law replied, 'and I am frightened.'

And all night long, they heard the agitated voice of Munashe from the adjacent hut admonishing Chenai that she had stalled his plans to return to Mozambique by advising people from his home that he had returned from the war. There was now no way that he would ever free himself of the ghosts of war that haunted him and he would never forgive her for that.

Several years later, the two women, *Amai* Mujuru and her sister-in-law, made several futile attempts to reflect on what exactly had transpired at what was supposed to be a historic reunion with Munashe who had been away for nearly a decade but each time they tried, they were confronted with the same awkward futility, the same painful emptiness in his eyes, his voice hollow and rasping through the dark night repeating that he wanted to return to Mozambique to find his bearings. But they both admitted that this was the day when they realized that the man had become a stranger to them. Was that the legacy of the war? Was this what everyone was reaping for their efforts? And this was when they stopped seeing the celebrations taking place wildly around them because they were more concerned with the problem that had afflicted their home.

'We must help him,' his sister-in-law said determinedly.

But what they found inhibiting was that although Munashe accepted there was something wrong with him, he did not believe it was as serious as they said it was. So that when he finally arrived home in Mhondoro a week later, there was not the intoxicating home-coming ceremony with bleary-eyed villagers from the surrounding homes, only the guarded whispers that his father exchanged with his young brother and mother. But Munashe was already worried about something else, about how unfamiliar the country looked and the suspicious glances that the otherwise ordinary villagers cast upon him: why did everyone seem to think that there was something wrong with him? He was right. If it was not for Chenai, he would have quietly sorted out his problem. Damn Chenai. And then he thought of Kudzai and the image of her dead, naked body down by the dry riverbed between Base One and Three at Chimoio after the attack by the South African commandos. It tormented him and he knelt down and embraced her.

'Are you crazy?' chided a fellow guerrilla standing over him. 'Can't you see her skin is peeling! And the foul smell! Shit.'

Munashe stood back and saw the mutilated breasts and the twisted legs and the blood smudges between the thighs and the single bullet hole through the forehead. But above all, he saw anger that only he could understand in her half-closed eyes and the impudent scowl on her blood-spattered lips. And he knew she had not died silently.

'The bastards raped her before killing her!' the other guerrilla said angrily. 'Let's go!' he shouted but Munashe remained standing, looking down at the angry corpse of his beloved Kudzai wondering what sort of fate it was that comdemned her to a life of perpetual rape. It seemed it was all that she had ever really known of the war and it was ironically the last ritual that she endured before her unceremonious death.

'Let's get away from here!' Munashe's colleague shouted at him, from behind a clump of bushes. Munashe slung his AK over his shoulder and followed him. He did not look back because he was afraid she might sit up and accuse him, asking him if this was what all that they had known of each other amounted to, and of course the promise, her promise. And as he walked further and further away from her angry decomposing corpse, he did not feel any anger over the humiliation and pain that she had suffered in her brief life, but instead a fear and despicable pity for himself. He was afraid that all the people he had known and even loved in the war were falling one after the other by the wayside whilst strangely he carried on, as if his survival was nurtured by their spilt blood. When would his day come? And then he felt the sharp pain stab his shoulder-blade, as the bullet ate through the shoulder that night at Mount Selinda and he doubled up.

The battle to overrun Mount Selinda which lay face to face with the small Mozambican town of Espungabeira was of no military significance at all, only a huge political booster. Instruction had come down the ranks that because of the impending political negotiations which were to be brokered by either the British or the Americans, the guerrillas' bargaining position would be strengthened if they brought along any white political prisoners. The attack was a joint operation with FRELIMO, as the latter blasted artillery fire from multiple mounted rocket launchers and recoilless rifles inside Mozambique and the guerrillas provided front line fire and close combat. The battle for the small town began just after sunset and the dark night exploded with small arms and artillery fire and there was pandemonium as the residents of the otherwise sleepy hamlet ran helter-skelter in the dark, trying to understand what was happening to them. Munashe's section was in the leading stick and came in from the southern side of the town but this it seemed was the side on which the Rhodesians had mounted their stiffest resistance because it was the side on which the offices of the Special Branch were located.

By the time they reached the offices, they had been abandoned and there was nothing left but a heavy pall of gunpowder smoke. They could hear desperate screams as people rushed about confusedly in the dark. And then there was a barrage of gunfire from somewhere and Munashe felt searing pain and he fell, so he did not hear his fellow comrades return fire and silence the Special Branch snipers. But perhaps the most exciting part that he missed was the short-lived celebration as the guerrillas triumphantly shook hands with the residents of the small town during the brief time that they had liberated it before the Rhodesian garrison recovered from the surprise attack, regrouped and hit back. If he had not been injured, he would also have known that they had not brought back any prisoners of war, black or white. He only regained consciousness on a makeshift stretcher as he was ferried across the border to the sound of the Rhodesian artillery whining across the dark sky above them and he felt an enormous bolt of pain emanating from the base of his shoulder and surging upwards through the roof of his skull. It was then that he realized there was a curious similarity between the acute pain that had engulfed him and his love for Kudzai. And when he tried, a long time after the war, to explain the strange similarity between these two unrelated emotions, it only helped to confirm their suspicion that he was mad.

He thought of her intensely at the dilapidated military clinic at Espungabeira with its inadequate medical supplies until he did not know whether he was suffering or enjoying the memory. They would float together in his pain, drifting between the clouds, softly touching the woollen edges and then tearing the clouds apart and tossing the fleecy pieces into the air around them and watching the wind push the pieces away and then sail after them and touch them again, whilst below them the horrible war raged on. What a reprieve!

She came to see him at Chimoio Hospital, to which he was finally transferred, and she held his hand in hers for a long time and he did not know whether it was a continuation of his dream in the clouds at Espungabeira or not and he said:

'If you hadn't kept holding my hand at Espungabeira, I would have died.'

And she squeezed his hand gently in hers because she knew he had at last arrived from the land of his strange dreams. 'I have been coming here every day since you arrived four days ago. How are you feeling?'

'Four days! But I only came here this morning!'

'Never mind,' she said and kissed him softly on his forehead. 'The bastard died at the front! He was threatening to kill you. I was afraid to tell you.'

'Who died at the front?' he asked.

'Never mind,' she said absent-mindedly and bent down and kissed him again gently on the forehead and he saw the dimple on her left cheek and he whispered:

'You saved me. I don't know how to thank you.'

And about a month later as he recuperated at Parirenyatwa, the medical base of the sprawling constellation of camps at Chimoio, she said:

'War is strange. Nothing is guaranteed. All the people we see today may be gone tomorrow.' She paused. Then: 'We might all be gone tomorrow,' she added prophetically. 'Now may be all the time that we have together.'

'Don't be so damn pessimistic.'

'I'm not saying the war will soon be over. I am merely saying that we may soon be gone forever. The war will always be there. It will outlive the rest of us.'

'And when the war finally comes to an end and we are lucky enough to be there, I wonder what sort of people we will be then.' He had laughed. She had also laughed. They were both laughing at the preposterous possibility.

'When the war is over and you go home, I want you to go and tell my father and mother and brothers and sister in Norton that there was no way that I could have survived.'

'Stop acting crazy, Kudzai!'

'Tell them I died here.'

And a month later, Kudzai died down by the dry riverbed and as Munashe walked blindly away from her naked, mutilated body, he hated himself and the only relief that he could think of was to return to the front and plunge himself in more blood-letting to cleanse himself of the guilt that he felt over her death, as if there could have been anything he could do not only to save her, but the scores of others who had died in the early morning bombardment.

He had survived by instinct using that invaluable knowledge, so difficult to quantify and describe, that he had accumulated over his years at the front. He had smeared himself with the blood of his dead comrades and lain motionless among dead bodies in the devastated bush hospital; he had even had the audacity to open an eye and observe the heavy boots of the South African commandos as they rolled bodies over, thudding from room to room, shoving paper into their knapsacks, swearing in deep monosyllabic Afrikaans, and it reminded him of the commandos bathing many years ago in the Mazoe River, as they desperately lunged for their rifles, and the sharp burst of his AK halting them forever, only now the constantly shifting positions of war had been reversed.

And Munashe's desire to go back to the front was heightened during the weeks following the release of military and political leaders from jail in Zambia where they had been incarcerated after the death of Chairman Chitepo. Suddenly there had been

108

dark talk of purges and the arrest of military commanders who were alleged to have been plotting a coup and Munashe was reminded of the dark days that preceded the death of Chairman Chitepo when he was unwittingly caught up in the fray and asked to batter to death the woman with the baby on her back because she was a wife of one of the dissidents and the following morning, even before he had fully recovered, he jumped into the first Land Rover back to the front. He would rather fight at the front than be dragged into the cruel and destructive wrangles in the camps with Ian Smith having the last laugh in Milton Building. And he heard from Bikita, Bocha, Buhera, Marange, the nauseating groans from the camps at the rear inside Mozambique as history flipped back through its pages to the internal mass arrests, the torture, the detention and even the executions, and Munashe made the shameless resolution that, come what may, the war that he was going to fight would be for no one else but Kudzai and the other woman with the crying baby on her back whom he had battered to death for something that he did not know had happened, to atone for their deaths which represented the chilling absurdity of war.

So that as he walked distractedly along the dry, sand-filled streams that wove through his home in Mhondoro, after they had taken him away from Chimanda, he wondered what had happened to the bruised land. It lay on its side looking visibly sick. Where had the false-medlar, the ebony and the spiny-leaved monkey orange trees gone? Where were the masked weavers with their intricate nests overlooking silent pools? Where were the song thrushes perched on swaying lucky-bean branches? Where was their chorus of funereal song? Where were the silent kingfishers watching the rolling world from the top of a branch? Where was the ugly, primordial candelabra tree that his grandfather had told him was the staple food of the equally primordial rhinoceros?

And then he began to see Kudzai, standing in the veld in front of him, picking ripe ebony fruit, mischievously biting off the peel and offering him the juicy flesh. And then he floated towards her to receive the gift but before he could hold her outstretched hand she dissolved into thin air and he was left clutching at nothing. And then he heard her call out his name from the top of an old *musasa* tree, beckoning him to climb up and join her, and he clambered up afraid that he might again find her gone and just as before, she dissolved into air and he was left with nothing but a memory. And then he saw them, Kudzai and a blurred field operational commander, he could not make out which one, standing at the top of the rise. Kudzai was struggling to free herself from his grip whilst he looked lasciviously down upon her, his mouth twisted into a cruel smile, and Munashe rushed up to them in blind rage and then the blurred field commander threw her fighting body over his shoulders and disappeared behind the rise. What Munashe found so hard was his failure to make out who the man was. He scrambled up after them, scrambled to the place where they had been standing and shading his eyes with his hands, peered down the incline but he could not see anyone, only several small boys herding cattle by the dry stream.

There was a small hill to the east of the village with two naked boulders rising from its crown which looked down upon the barren land below. He called the smaller boulder Kudzai and the bigger one, himself. Each sunset, he climbed up the hill and sat on the bigger boulder, and felt Kudzai beside him as they both silently watched the village below prepare to sleep. They were silent not because they did not have anything to talk about; they were convalescing from too many painful memories. They sat silent, listening to their anguish and waiting for the moon to rise. Then she would raise her eyes and point at the woman carrying a baby on her back inside the moon:

'I understand why you did it,' she soothed him. 'Let's say a short prayer to placate her. It was the war.'

He stretched his trembling hand and touched her.

She raised her eyes and smiled at him and once again he saw the dimple on her cheek and kissed her. Meanwhile, his mother and father, indeed everyone else in the village, looked at him and sorrowfully shook their heads. The war had delivered them an unnegotiable gift.

Years afterwards, Kudzai's young sister, Chipo, who later became his wife, asked him why it had taken him so long to go to Norton and tell Kudzai's family about her death, as she had requested that he do for her.

'I could not come and tell you about the death of someone who I was then living with. Kudzai was alive to me. Otherwise I should have died a long time ago.'

Chipo shrugged her shoulders and looked at her mother who stared out through the window, pretending not to hear the discussion between her daughter and her husband. She found it so difficult that fate could be so cruel as to bind the destinies of her only two daughters to this man who was, as it were, thrown on them by the prowling ghost of a horrible war.

In time he would reluctantly admit to himself that in all his tortured, aimless wandering after the war, he had not postponed anything as much as that journey to Norton. It was a journey that he was frightened to undertake, as if it would confirm his growing awareness that there was after all something seriously wrong with him: Kudzai was indeed dead.

'Who are you?' Kudzai's mother asked, looking curiously at the man, the first time that he had arrived in their home in Norton.

'I am a long story,' Munashe replied. 'You will never be able to understand it.'

'You are saying Kudzai died at Chimoio and you were with her?' the old woman said, shaking her head. And then Chipo came in from the kitchen and stared at the mysterious stranger, dredged up from the war years.

'At 88 Manica Road they told us she was doing advanced military training in Romania!' she challenged.

'Kudzai was killed in an early morning attack on Chimoio during the war. I was there.'

Chipo shook her head and walked out of the room, and as she averted her face towards the sun shining through the open window, Munashe saw the small dimple in her left cheek. It was not quite as pronounced as Kudzai's, but there was a striking resemblance between the two girls, and he started as if haunted.

Chipo sold fish that she bought from the fishing co-operatives around Lakes Mhanyame and Chivero and he began to help her; it became his first meaningful engagement after the war. He woke up early in the morning every day, long before his brother-in-law, vaMujuru, and caught the first emergency taxi to Norton and by the time she arrived at the lake, he would already have put aside the fish that she would buy. Then they would sell the fish to passing motorists along the Bulawayo Road. What she found fascinating about him, that is besides his reluctant stories, was his obsession with work. He worked as if he was possessed. When he was preoccupied, he called her Kudzai and she found that amusing, at least at first. In a very short time she was surprised to realize how much about him she knew; she felt that probably no one else knew as much. The responsibility weighed on her but as there was nothing she could do, she shrugged her shoulders, and accepted it.

'Women seemed to have been helpless in the war, not allowed to make any decisions, exercise any choice. The woman with the baby on her back was powerless and even my sister seemed helpless!'

'But sometimes they made strange choices,' he said and he told her about an incident in the killing fields of Buhera. Muzorewa had by then entered the war with his armed Pfumo Revanhu. It seemed that practically the whole country was armed when they got embroiled in a vicious fire-fight near a school in Murambinda. Munashe shouted at the students, especially the girls, to lie down otherwise they would get shot. And then he had turned, he did not know why, and saw one of the lady teachers whip a pistol out and shoot Comrade Granger, who was kneeling next to him, through the back of his head. The man had stumbled and fallen down flat on his face, the collar of his shirt blooming flower-red. Then the woman had swung her gun towards Munashe; he had seen it all in a moment. His response was automatic as he turned his AK on her and she fell in a heap under a barrage of gunfire.

'What strange thing is happening in Norton?' his sister asked one evening, seeing that his eyes were shining and full of life.

'Nothing,' he answered.

*Va*Mujuru put aside the paper he was reading and looked at him, smiling mischievously. 'When shall we be graced by her honour, whoever she is?'

Munashe looked at him and smiled and when his sister saw his smile, tears filled her eyes. It was the first time she had seen her brother smile since his return.

'How could I have not thought you were a God-send?' she confessed to Chipo a few years later. 'You brought him back to life.'

Meanwhile, Chipo's mother sighed, wondering what fate had bound the destinies of her only two girls to a man who like the war itself would surely wreak havoc on the lives of others. But as she watched the man's personality rub off on her daughter she reluctantly admitted that she was powerless to stop anything

113

happening. The young woman had closed her eyes, and was waiting for him to take her wherever he wanted.

'I love him. He only needs a stable job. We are looking out for one, Mother. Afterwards, he might go back to university. If you had any idea of the things they made people do out there, you would cry.'

'They enjoyed cutting off people's ears and then forcing the victims to eat them. Who doesn't know that? They were psychopaths!'

And when the woman with the baby on her back finally arrived, there was pandemonium not only in the hut, but in the whole village. It had begun with Munashe waking up violently and looking around with wild eyes. Then he had leapt out of the hut and fled in the direction of the cattle pens. His father had run after him but Manhokwe had grabbed the old man from behind and dragged him back into the hut, admonishing him.

'Where do you think you are going, boy without hair on the crotch? Let the woman with the baby on her back come to pass.'

And then she had thrown her voice into the lead of a song full of anguish:

> *Ndagonei wenyu wauya*
> *zidzikana risinawo kana hama*
> *tambirai mose*

And the lead mbira player stood up and craned his neck, pulling his muscles forward as if he wanted to catch sight of something hidden in the darkness around him. The drummer half-stood, holding the drum firmly between his cracked knees, and listened intently to the magic that his flashing hands moulded on the taut ox-hide of the throbbing instrument. And then he smiled. He knew from his vast experience of facilitating communication between people of this world and that other beyond

114

the sky that the ceremony was about to reach its climax and explode: the two worlds were about to collide.

Ndagonei, what can I possibly do right? the tormented wandering spirit in the song was calling for help from the outskirts of an unknown village, theirs. She had been wandering from place to place without sleep and shelter for years. She was tired and could hardly drag her bruised feet another step. She wanted a place where she could rest her head. But above all, she wanted to give some rest to the baby crying on her lacerated back. And above the anguishing words of the song, they heard Munashe bellow from behind the cattle pens because he was the woman with the baby on her back and he wanted to be received into the village for a brief respite from the cold and hunger and pain and exhaustion. And then he approached the village and stood on top of the anthill to the east and cried out in anguish, his frame shaped against the yellowing eastern horizon:

I want a moment's rest under the shade of the musasa *tree in the middle of the home to breast-feed my baby. I beg you not to reject me.*

And the village heard the heart-rending cry because there was no way that the small ritual at *va*Mungate's home could be contained there any longer and from somewhere down the line of homesteads, they heard a booming howl, hoom hoom hoom, and everyone knew that Mberera, *va*Shekede's baboon spirit had arrived and ululations from several huts all over the village broke echoing into the air and there was nothing to understand.

Munashe was finally brought under the canopy of the *musasa* tree in the middle of the homestead, writhing to the fierce rhythm of the music, and Manhokwe leapt into the air in front of the procession, throwing fistfuls of soil into the air, menacingly baring her canines at Mberera sneaking in from the sides, and the baboon whimpered and scuttled away.

'Who are you?' Manhokwe asked after the music had died away at last.

Munashe, his face cast down, as if he was shy to look into their faces, was gently rocking some imaginary burden on his back.

'I asked who you are.' Manhokwe asked again, her voice slightly raised.

Then Munashe raised his face and looked around. 'How can you ask me such a question?' he challenged in a thin and tremulous voice. 'I didn't know what it was like here; the people, the village. Please give me some water, my throat is parched.'

'Who are you?' Manhokwe asked angrily.

'How can you ask such a question as if you don't know who I am? Oo-o, how glad I am to have arrived. I am tired of wandering. My whole life has been spent wandering in the wilderness. Now I have returned.'

'We want to take you home. Who are you and where do you come from?'

'Which home do you mean? What other home?' she challenged.

Several months later when the drama was over, Chipo would confess to her mother that she no longer knew what to believe. 'The difference between the story of the Rhodesian rifleman who helped him secure a job in Mutare and that of the arrival of the woman with the baby on her back was that I had only heard the first one. I saw the other one happening in front of my eyes. There was the man I knew so well, sitting in the middle of the gathering, as day broke in the eastern sky, speaking in a female voice. At first I thought he was feigning it but as I watched him gently rock a baby on his back as the woman inside him related the details of her death, I could no longer bear it and I began to cry.'

'You know who I am and where my home is,' the woman said, taking the crying baby off her back and putting it to her breast.

Mberera, the baboon, snivelled from the periphery of the compound to attract attention but the lioness growled at it and the baboon, cowering, clambered up the *musasa* tree under whose canopy they were sitting and someone quipped that the baboon could steal the occasion and shamelessly become the centre of attraction, and several people stifled nervous laughter.

On a brief visit to her sister-in-law's in Rugare a few weeks after the event, *Mai* Taurayi would rebuke her husband's behaviour.

'I still can't understand my husband. What *still* seems to irk him most, is his car! Imagine that!' she said.

'Has it been towed from Nyautare yet?' *Amai* Mujuru asked.

'It was returned last week. Imagine he blames the trip on *Baba* and says he is still in two minds whether to make him pay for the repairs or not.'

'I hadn't known Jonathan was that heartless!'

'He is still furious that the trip to the home of the woman with the baby on her back was one that he was forced into, and with all those people. What happened to his 404 station-wagon is something he will never forgive.'

'How can his 404 be more important than anything else?' The two women shrugged their shoulders, unable to comprehend such behaviour.

Much later that morning after the strange visitations, the village lay withdrawn and sorrowful, as if a funeral was about to take place. A cloud hung over *va*Mungate's home. The mbira players under the huge *musasa* silently packed their bags and equipment before they left in single file for their homes, the sun behind them. Their leader kept shaking his head and mumbling that in all his years in the business, he had not known anything like it. What had prompted him to refuse payment for the night's performance was the early morning discovery of lion footprints

117

around the village. Where had the lions come from? Surely not from the overcrowded, barren communal areas where even finding a hare was considered a miracle? He was so disturbed that even as he walked he kept asking himself whether he could ever be involved in another performance like the one they had just experienced. *Va*Mungate stood behind his granary, his arms folded across his chest, looking thoughtfully into the horizon. *Va*Nyagadzi tottered on her walking stick from the bushes behind the cattle pens. And inside the hut, where the pandemonium had spilled over, *Amai* Mujuru dozed beside the dead fire-place. Her sister-in-law, *Amai* Taurayi, tapped gently to the rhythm of the music inside her head on one of the hearthstones. And Munashe lay asleep as his wife dabbed his forehead with a piece of wet cloth. The man had developed a mysterious fever.

PART THREE

All the way from Harare to Nyautare lying at the foot of Nyangani Mountain, a mountain shrouded with mystery and stories of people who had disappeared without trace in its thick swirling mists; all the way past the small farming town of Marondera wondering whether it would be able to escape Harare's increasingly domineering shadow; and on past cheeky Macheke making faces at passing motorists because they never stopped to sample her simple delights; all the way past Eagle's Nest, caught within a plantation of swaying blue gums; and on past Rusape, curled up trying to catch some sleep, exhausted from the previous night's reckless drinking; all the way north along the steeply winding road, climbing higher and higher, leaving valleys, gulleys and ravines below; all the way past Montclair Hotel famous for its permanent nocturnal escapades by gamblers and fortune seekers at its casinos and fruit-machines; and on past dappled apple and peach orchards clinging to the mountain sides; and on past the dainty little town of Nyanga sitting cross-legged at the top of the rise, drifting mists and piles of fluffy clouds massed low in the sky above; and then down a gravel road to the north following the foot of the range of mountains that stretched into the horizon. And then the country started to wither, and so on through arid terrain where gaping huts obediently followed the winding road; first one dilapidated country school, and then another; and on across an old bridge, meeting an old bus driving from the north and getting lost in the swirling dust left in its wake, going on and on and on forever past thin cattle grazing in the sun and the unbroken stare of silent villagers. Jonathan sat sullen and silent, hunched behind the steering wheel, staring straight ahead, his shirt stuck to his back,

119

occasionally sipping the lager grasped between his legs and sulking on a journey that seemed never to end.

Munashe, sandwiched between his wife and *vatete* Nyagadzi at the back of the station-wagon, fought to shrug off his splitting headache and he thought about the mystery that shrouded the mountain. Strange stories were told of people claiming to have sighted armed guerrillas disappearing into the mist that enveloped the mountains. The various claims, however bizarre, seemed to be linked by strange coincidence: in all the versions the guerrillas never talked to each other because there was nothing any longer to talk about; they kept their faces turned to the mist to be sure that no one recognized them; they were always on the move. Debate raged as to who these men were. Some people said they were the dregs of a war which they did not know had ended. Others said they were the wandering ghosts of fallen combatants who did not want anybody to see that they were crying.

There were also other strange stories about what had happened in the mountains. Two daughters of a prominent politician had disappeared without trace during a walk up the mountain and, in spite of a massive search by the army, the police and the air force, they were never found. Once again, debate raged as people tried to explain their mysterious disappearance. Some people thought the girls had lost their way in a sudden blanketing mist and fallen down a bottomless cliff which not even air force helicopters could reach. Others thought the girls had been abducted by armed elements of RENAMO and taken back to Mozambique. And yet a third group thought the girls had decided to join the group of wandering guerrillas and become their companions. And then there was also the possibility that Mtwarazi, the legendary mountain spirit, might have whisked them away to add to his legion of wives, a theory given strength by the complete lack of any

120

evidence; the girls might have simply disappeared into the thin misty air.

Munashe looked at the mountains and remembered when he had looked at them from deep inside Mozambique. He found it strange that several years after the end of the war, he would travel along the foot of the same mountains, inside his country, looking for the woman with the baby on her back in order to exorcise the ghosts that haunted him. And then he glanced into the car's rearview mirror and his eyes met with the tired, hostile eyes of his brother and the younger man looked away and Munashe wondered what he was thinking about. Silence. A long heavy unbroken silence had accompanied them all the way from Harare.

And then *Mai* Taurayi pointed at a hill rising to the west, a stunted baobab sitting on its crown, and she gasped, 'There!'

Munashe's mother looked at the hill and sighed. *Va*Mungate, sitting beside her, mumbled something inaudible and looked the other way. Jonathan stole a glance at the baobab and silently cursed his brother.

Munashe raised his eyes, saw the hill and felt a strange numbness steal through his mind and body. Then a shadow hovered on the horizon of his mind and disappeared and he was filled with despair. He did not hear his wife exclaim:

'And there!' pointing at the smaller kopje not far away which the lioness had also told them was the weaned child of the divorced woman who carried the huge baobab tree on her head. A long time ago, so the legend went, Dodzo was married to the great Nyangani Mountain hovering not far to the east. Then a misunderstanding arose between them and in spite of the intervention of the sisters of the great mountains, several hills across the border inside Mozambique, the husband chased the wife away from his home and divorced her. Because she was an

121

orphan, the wife had nowhere to go. So she stood dejectedly outside the royal village with her suckling baby and cried, hoping that one day the king would feel pity for her. And ever since, she had been standing there weeping to an unheeding monarch, and hoping that one day when her son was old enough to understand, he would plead with his father to accept them back into the royal village.

And then Jonathan, still sulking, looked for a suitable place and parked the vehicle at the bottom of the hill where they could see the village in the valley below. There they waited for night to fall, as that was when the lioness had told them something would happen.

It was the herd boys driving their animals home from the pastures who saw the strangers first and they stopped and gazed at them. The word travelled rapidly down the valley and the old village stirred and looked with suspicion at the silent strangers gathered at the foot of the hill. And there was a flurry of movement as the elders of the village consulted with the headman and the golden rays of the setting sun slanted across the valley and bounced off the sides of the large slumbering mountain to the east and the two shadows belonging to the mountain's wife and son stealthily crept up its flanks as if they were trying to steal their way back into the village out of banishment and Munashe felt numb and a silence thicker than the dark night descended upon the village while the strangers gathered at the foot of the hill continued to wait as they had been instructed and Jonathan took a blanket from the boot of the car and, cursing under his breath, threw it on the ground and resting his aching head on the worn-out spare wheel seemed to doze off.

Then they heard a high-pitched wail from the village down the valley and it broke the night into a thousand pieces and *va*-Nyagadzi tensed and shook her head vigorously, emitting a deep-throated grunt as if she was in great pain. And then the wailing continued and the slumbering mountain angrily hurled the doomed cry back down the valley as if it knew that the village could have sent it a more promising message and there were many voices in the dark and *va*Nyagadzi continued to shake violently and Munashe felt the numbness spread slowly over his body, paralyzing him, and then he heard a deafening explosion and saw great balls of fire erupt as the Vampires and Hawks screamed across the sky and he threw himself down as the dreaded choppers, nicknamed the Poachers, emerged suddenly from behind the hills, pounding the guerrilla positions to smithereens, and he fired wildly and watched the muzzle of his AK turn red-hot and his nostrils were clogged with the sickening smell of gunpowder and he became mad and hurled insults at the flying monsters, the fucking war, and then his wife shook him violently and he woke up, soaked in sweat. She calmly stood up and switched on the lights.

'It's the nightmares again?' she asked.

'Yes!' he answered breathlessly.

'The war is over, my husband,' she whispered into his ear, stroking his head gently.

'These bad dreams will eventually go away of their own accord,' he said as he sat up on the creaking bed and gulped down a mugful of water. She looked at him for a long time, sighed, and turned the other way. Silence fell.

Then the wailing down in the village stopped and several men clapped their hands and a woman ululated and then the voice of another woman broke into song:

> *Ko pane angandiudzewo here*
> *Chakatemura muzukuru wangu?*
> *Ndiani angandirumewo nzeve*

Kwakaendwa nomwana womwana wangu?
Vamwe vanoti ambuya
Muzukuru akarumwa nenyoka.
Vamwe vachiti ambuya
Chizukuru chakaitwa zvokupondwa.

She sang of the victim's grandmother repeatedly asking the same question: can anyone tell me what happened to my granddaughter? can anybody tell me what ate my granddaughter? and the futile responses by various people conjecturing what might have happened to the young woman: *ambuya*, the young woman was lost without trace in the mountain mists; grandmother, the girl died from a mamba's lethal strike; *ambuya*, the woman was murdered and then hanged to hide the heinous act.

And at the foot of the hill the lioness leapt into the air and raced up the hill, its face averted from the moon peeping over the top of the mountain to the east and the roar echoed and re-echoed in the surrounding hills: Manhokwe, who had promised them that she would follow them to Nyanga, had at last arrived. And there was a frightening stand-off as the village asked repeatedly what had happened to its daughter who had gone to the war and never come back and the lioness, prowling around the baobab tree at the top of the hill, roared back menacingly, baring its canines, and the silver light of the moon draped the surrounding hills and Munashe's wife exclaimed at the woman with the baby on her back inside the moon because she had never previously noticed that the woman carried a bundle of firewood on her head.

A long time later, when the moonlight had reached the village and flooded the valley and the huge naked boulders in the hills and mountains had grown cold to the touch, a delegation of three men was sent from the village to quiz the strangers gathered at the foot of the hill.

124

'Who are you? Where do you come from? What do you want?'

'We are strangers to this part of the land,' replied *va*Mungate, his head lowered, clapping his hands in greeting. 'We have been led here by the spirit of the lioness,' he jerked his head towards the top of the hill where the lioness roared. 'We are on a sorrowful mission to search for the home at which to lay the invisible burden we are carrying.'

And the lioness roared whilst the village continued to ask angrily what had happened to its daughter who never returned from the war and, without saying another word, the three envoys stood up and brushed the backsides of their worn trousers with their scarred hands and filed back to the village and it was only after midnight that the uninvited visitors were asked to come down and they trailed wearily along a path down into the valley with *va*Mungate leading the straggling group and Jonathan, sulking, closed the rear and the lioness followed them down the hill and prowled round at the edge of the village in slow circles and the mangy village dogs bayed at the strangers but carefully kept their distance and the whole village gathered at the home of the spirit medium who was also the wife of the headman and the night's mysterious proceedings began and there was nothing to understand.

Then the spirit medium who was also the wife of the headman and the grandmother of the young woman with the baby on her back asked them the question that the three men who had been sent to the foot of the hill had asked, the men who had later quietly brushed their worn-out trousers with their scarred hands, and *va*Mungate clapped his hands, his head lowered to the ground, and then cleared his throat but before he would say anything, Munashe fell into convulsions, frothing at the corners of his dry mouth, and then he suddenly sat up and looked at the people gathered around.

'It's been such a long, long journey. I am glad I have finally arrived home. I haven't seen Mother yet, where is she? Mother, your daughter Rudo has finally come home from the war.' He looked around and then turned and looked at an old man with a bald head sitting near the door. 'Father, I have not returned from the war empty-handed. I have brought you a small gift,' and he proceeded to unstrap the invisible baby on his back. 'Your grandchild's name is Hondo. He is my gift to you. All the time I spent out there was not spent in vain,' and he began to rock and cuddle the invisible baby, cooing a lullaby into its ear. 'After so much pain, isn't this good news?' he laughed a little carelessly.

Someone in the gathering began to weep and the spirit medium of the village who also happened to be the wife of the headman who was also the grandmother of the woman with the baby on her back snapped at her to stop crying because she was foolish and they required everyone to remain calm and collected; if she began when the proceedings were so young, where then would she be when the day finally dawned? There was silence except for the agitated voice of Manhokwe prowling in the dark outside the village and the desperate baying of the mangy village dogs and vaMungate broke the silence in the room:

'This is the reason why we of the Shumba totem have come all the way from the land without trees in Mhondoro to your land of mountains that touch the sky.' And he jerked his head towards Munashe and then clapped his hands and the sound echoed in the crowded room and there was another silence.

The man with the bald head sitting next to the door made a sound in his throat and turned: 'What exactly happened in Mozambique during the war?' he asked. There was an unsettling rasp in his voice.

'Let's hold our dogs on the leash!' intervened the spirit medium

126

of the village who was also the grandmother of the young woman with the baby on her back.

After a long pause, his eyes still cast down to the ground, *va*Mungate slowly took them through the shocking details of Rudo and her child's death at the remote guerrilla base inside Mozambique at the height of the war more than a decade ago and the people listened in horrified silence and somewhere in the dark, several women choked as they fought back the crying trapped inside their chests but the enormous one inside Rudo's mother, hidden behind the other women, broke loose and she went down on all fours and crawled in front of Munashe and the tears fell from her eyes and the woman lamented:

'Is this you Rudo, my daughter? Is this how you have decided to come back to your mother? Is this the grandchild that you promised you would bear for me a long time ago when you were still at school?' And then turning to the spirit medium of the village who was also the wife of the headman, she mourned: 'Is this our harvest for all our effort during the war? Is this the harvest we are reaping after all our pain and sacrifice? Is this our reward for sleepless nights, and all the shooting and the dying in the dark?'

And then the man with the bald head sitting next to the door, in a surprising about-turn, half stood and barked at the woman, who was also his wife, to close her foul mouth immediately because she was offending not only the living but also the dead. But the woman could not be deterred so easily. She turned and looked angrily at her husband, a silhouette etched against the lean moonlight coming through the door.

'I am not saying all this to be compensated. Neither am I asking anybody to bring my daughter back to life. I am saying what I am saying to ease the pain within me.' And then she collapsed on Munashe's lap and wailed like the small child that

127

her daughter would have brought back from the war if she had survived and several people, both men and women, cried in the dark and Munashe continued to rock the invisible baby in his arms and outside, the lioness roared with renewed vigour and the mangy village dogs bayed even more desperately.

'You can't blame the woman,' a man's voice shouted from the dark. 'Neither can you blame these people from Mhondoro. Would anybody say they had got anything out of the war?' he asked, waving his hand at Munashe. 'They are as helpless and tortured as we are,' he paused. 'It's not as if we expected much. But this!' again he pointed at Munashe and made a clicking noise. 'Perhaps the only people left whom we can ask to wash away our pain are those beyond the sky.' He looked at the village spirit medium who was also the wife of the headman and the grand-mother of the young woman with the baby on her back.

The spirit medium laughed derisively. 'What with all the drought, and the strange new incurable disease, and the dark shadows stealing across the land, none of us understand what's happening down here any longer. All we do is gather every day not to pray but to weep for those of you left behind. I am glad you realize that you can't blame these people from the land of vast and open plains. Your problem and their problem is the same.' And her voice trailed away into the dark night.

And then, suddenly, Munashe sprang up like a whirlwind and crashed out of the hut and disappeared into the night running towards the great mountain, the lioness and the village dogs behind him.

'It was all so unexpected,' his wife would tell the finance manager at Mutare Timbers a few days afterwards. 'With every-one weeping or saying one thing or the other, he had calmed down and I rested his head on my lap. Then I felt a violent movement growing inside him and I held him down firmly but the seizures kept growing stronger and stronger and he broke loose and leapt out of the hut. In that brief moment as I tried to hold him down, I could feel that he was no longer the man that I once knew. He had become ... a monster.' She looked away. And when the finance manager at last raised his eyes from the ground, she saw the tears that he had fought to hold back.

But that night at the village in the valley near the mountain, everyone scrambled out of the hut and peered into the darkness in the direction of the baying dogs which Munashe never heard. After a brief chase, the dogs returned. The lioness too but the man ran on, over the hills and the mountains, through forests and more forests. He ran until daybreak and he came to a river and on the other side of the water was someone that he thought he remembered. He peered more closely. The man had the bazooka dangling at his side. Comrade Bazooka!

Was he dreaming?

'There is a crossing point a short distance down the river,' he said in that crisp, unmistakable voice that Munashe would always recognize. And indeed, there was a footbridge not far away. As he crossed the river, he felt a strange sensation: as if he were being born again. And once on the other side, he felt a new man and he could feel the light in his eyes and the spring in his stride. And he saw that sunshine hung languidly in the air and he touched it and held it in his hands and then he blew it away. There was something magical about the atmosphere although he had the unsettling feeling that it would not last forever.

'She sent me to come and wait for you,' Bazooka said. Munashe did not ask who the woman was because he already knew.

They walked briskly towards a hill to the east and then he saw her, sitting under the shade of a huge *mukamba* tree: Kudzai, holding an AK rifle in her hands. He opened his arms and rushed towards her and she stood up to receive him and the sunlight accentuated her dimple and Munashe melted into her arms.

'What kept you away for so long?' she asked after a long long time but, still holding her, he was unable to say anything. 'Let's go, otherwise we will be late.' She pushed him away and led the way. And they walked in silence, hand in hand, Munashe saw the woman with the baby on her back staring at them and he froze.

'Don't worry about her,' Kudzai said. 'I talked it over with her the other day and she assured me that she has forgiven you.' She waved and the woman waved back.

'Are you not coming to see the baby?' the woman asked, indicating the sleeping baby on her back.

'Some other time,' Kudzai called back. And: 'Are you not coming to the rally?' The woman said she would follow soon.

'What rally?' Munashe asked.

'Chairman Chitepo and Jason Moyo are addressing a rally at Base Ten to announce fundamental policy changes to the struggle. It is a critical rally. The war has been going on for quite some time and there may be a need to review the whole strategy.' She looked at him. 'Otherwise we might fight forever.'

'But hasn't the war ended?' Munashe asked.

'Which war do you mean?'

Munashe threw his arms in the air and mumbled that he did not understand. And in the distance, he heard the voices of people singing revolutionary songs and the words articulated their determination to fight on until they had shaken off any form of oppression and he kept moving on behind Kudzai and he began to see familiar faces: Comrade Tonderayi, the pleasant section commander to whom he could not tell his story, Comrade Gondo, Comrade Sly, the commissar who deserted but never got back to Salisbury, the Rhodesian rifleman and they all waved, glad to see him. And Kudzai squeezed his hand gently and they smiled at each other, but she said:

'I love you but the struggle will always be there between us.'

And Chairman Chitepo's voice reverberated above the singing voices:

'Forward with the struggle!

Forward with the masses of Zimbabwe!

Pasi neudzvinyiriri!

Down with nepotism!

Down with tribalism!

Down with regionalism!

Down with corruption!

A luta continua!

The struggle continues!'

And then there was silence and Munashe looked through the milling crowd and he saw him at last, the Chairman, on the raised platform: grey hair and fiery eyes, in a pin-striped blue suit, lifting a clenched fist; and Jason Moyo standing next to him: suave, wearing a polo-neck and jacket, arms clasped in front of him and a far-away look in his eyes. And then the Chairman talked angrily of a series of monumental historical betrayals and he said that he and a few others were the living examples of such betrayals and Jason Moyo wondered how the politics, the wealth and the economy of the entire country was slowly becoming synonymous with the names of less than a dozen people and he asked how in such circumstances the struggle could not be said to have lost its way and the man went down on his knees and wept: Cry, Zimbabwe. Cry beloved country and the atmosphere became electric and Chitepo continued:

'It's shocking to see the reluctance that we have to tell even the smallest truth. Ours shall soon become a nation of liars. We lie to our wives. We lie to our husbands. We lie at work. We lie in parliament. We lie in cabinet. We lie to each other. And what is worst is that we have begun to believe our lies. What I fear most is that we will not leave anything to our children except lies and silence.'

Someone in the gathering began to weep and Munashe craned his neck to see what it was and he saw that it was Doctor Samuel Parirenyatwa, and Leopold Takawira, standing close by, put his arm round the weeping man and the Chairman continued:

'It all began with silence. We deliberately kept silent about some truths, no matter how small, because some of us felt that we would compromise our power. This was how the lies began because when we came to tell the history of the country and the history of the struggle, our silences distorted the story and made it defective. Then the silence spilled into the everyday lives of our people and translated itself into fear which they believe is the only protection that they have against imaginary enemies whom we have taught them to see standing behind their shoulders. They are no longer able to say what they want. Neither are they able to say what they think because they have become a nation of silent performers, miming their monotonous roles before an empty theatre. And behind the stage, we, their leaders, expend our energy, coining high-sounding words – indigenization, empowerment, smart-partnerships, affirmative action – with which we will silence them forever. We owe the people an explanation. The struggle continues.'

And Munashe looked at Kudzai:

'I do not understand.'

'You *should* understand better than most people here!' she said and Munashe shrugged his shoulders and looked away and his eyes met with those of the young woman with the baby on her back and stung with tears, and the woman walked over to him and patted him on the shoulder:

132

'It wasn't your fault,' she said.

And it was the villagers from an adjacent village who found his body the following morning lying in a gully at the foot of the mountain and they sent word around to find out who it was and when Munashe's wife finally arrived, she threw herself on the body and wept. The other women wailed, holding the back of their heads in their hands, looking towards the mountain as if it had something to do with his death, and the men cried silently, their heads lowered to the ground, their arms folded across their chests, occasionally shaking their heads. And Jonathan moved around as if he was a mad man.

His anger had started early in the morning when he had gone to his car and seen a puddle of oil beneath it: something, perhaps a stone, had rammed against the gearbox. But Jonathan had his own interpretation: if he hadn't been dragged to come all the way here, he wouldn't be in such a mess. And now this! He looked into the gully and saw the twisted body of his brother and he walked away. And the mountain looked down at them and two huge puddles of tears formed in its big eyes and it turned away. And the wife of the headman who was also the spirit medium of the village and the grandmother of the woman with the baby on her back thought that the man would always be remembered as the guerrilla fighter who brought two distant villages together to mourn in the strangest circumstances.

A day later, they sat silent at the back of the open truck sent from Mutare Timbers to ferry them back to Mhondoro. The police van in which his body had been placed travelled a short distance behind. They rode a rise and the hill with the squatting baobab came into full view and *Amai* Taurayi saw her husband moving in circles around his car, gesticulating to himself, occasionally kicking the car with his foot, and she was happy she was not there to listen to his grumbling and then she pushed him out of her mind and turned and looked at *vatete* Nyagadzi and remarked:

'At least, the war has ended for Munashe.'

'You think so?' *vatete* Nyagadzi asked philosophically.

'I warned him on the day that he left that the only thing that he would bring back, if he returned at all, was pain. Nothing else,' his sister, *Amai* Mujuru, said.

'I have never told anyone this before,' Munashe's wife said, looking into the distance. 'My sister, Kudzai, asked me in a dream to look after the gift that she had sent me from the war. I tried my best. You are right *Amai* Taurayi, the war has at last ended for him.' She looked away and began to cry. And they all wept save *vatete* Nyagadzi who silently went on chewing a blade of grass in her toothless mouth.

And down in the valley, the village lay silent and withdrawn, visibly shaken by the previous day's events and the discovery of the fresh footprints of lions around the village, and the elders shook their heads because they knew that things would never be the same again and the hill with the squatting baobab on its head held the hand of its son, looking anxiously across the valley at the child's slumbering father, yawning, throwing open his great, old jaws with more than half their teeth missing and the mother hoped that soon she would be accepted back into the village.

Glossary

Aizosunungurwa . . . pembe yenhunzi untied after blowing the whistle for flies

Amai ndinesimba . . . bu-u-u Mother I am strong and I will kill them

Ambuya grandmother

Baba Father

Bira propitiation ceremony

Chef term of respect for a superior, from the Portuguese for chief or leader, *chefe*

Chimurenga revolt

Chizarira trap

Dzepfunde we are listening

Mai Mother

Mbanje marijuana

Mbira Shona musical instrument considered to have mystical properties and used to invoke the ancestors

Mhunga sorghum

Mopani mopani tree, *Colophospermum mopane*

Mudhara old man

Mujibha young men and boys used by the guerrillas as scouts

Mukamba pod mahogany tree, *Afzelia quanzensis*

Mukoma brother

Mukuwasha brother-in-law

Mukuyu Cape fig tree, *Ficus sur*

135

Muonde   Cape fig tree, *Ficus sur*

Musasa   masasa tree, *Brachystegia spiciformis*

Mvura ishamwari yangu   the rain is my friend

Ndagonei wenyu . . . tambirai mose   your daughter Ndagonei has come, please receive her

Ndiri kuuya   I am coming

Nhai Mukuku mwanangu   listen Mukuku, my child

Pamberi nehondo   forward with the war

Pasi neudzvinyiriri   down with oppression

Pfumo rasvika   the enemy is approaching

Pindayi zvenyu   please come in

Shamwari   friend

Taireva   we said it

Tete or *Vatete*   auntie

Vanaamai . . . dzafunga kure   Mother and Father, who will you remain with when I am finally gone to the far away place in my mind?

Varidzi vesango . . . chezvishamiso   proprietor of the forest with eyes that light fire, mystery of mystery

Zvakati zvikati   a long time ago

Zvaonekwa Shumba . . . kumhepo ikoko   thank you great lion, please look after me in this wilderness as I fight the war